# LD100
## *KILL THEM ALL*

John E. Espy

OPEN
BOOKS

Published by Open Books

Cover image © alphaspirit.it shutterstock.com/g/alphaspirit.it/

Interior design by Siva Ram Maganti

*As always, I am grateful to my dear wife, Treasa Glinnwater for her continued love and support now through many years.*

# Chapter 1

WALKING IN BLOOD CAN'T help but reach down into the burrows of your soul and pull up thoughts of ghoul. Memories of that which frightened us as children are brought to bear in our moment-to-moment lives. Blood, if warm and fresh, is slick like ice, crimson ice. Walking through this kind of blood is always, one way or another, because someone has bled out right about the time the sole of your boot touches the ground. With each passing minute the blood begins to cool. Then each step is like walking through cold scarlet molasses.

She had never seen so much blood. Neither had anyone else unless they had been in war of course. Bodies, random bodies, splayed out in filthy beds, soaked in blood, piss and shit. Hospitals, if there were any, weren't the same as in the States. Here they were in the best of circumstances only a tent or two. The stakes pounded deep in the thick muck to keep the tent erect when the monsoonal winds come. Sometimes, the rain is so loud that it blessedly drowns out the screams of the dying. Unanswerable "*Help me's*" make the once firmed now forever infirmed.

But, now with the blood came the trembling, then the bones would sound like dried sticks. Snapping with a crack as those who were held in its intractable spell, muttered incomprehensibly. One couldn't even be sure if they felt their bones breaking. And the rash, the horrible rash that eventually became so prolific that it completely took over the person's skin.

Terror arose when they caught you with their increasingly keratinized eyes, frightened that you too would soon become possessed like them as they gazed pleadingly at you. The slack in the rope of hope rapidly becoming increasingly taut.

Their insides liquefying. If there wasn't an orifice for the blood to find its way out of, it would create one of its own, with the skin itself beginning to leach blood. "Jesus Christ," Isabella thought, "... *what* in the fuck is this?"

The tents were filling up with bodies. When she arrived, the sick were all in one tent. She had them separated. A staging. From one just showing symptoms to those hours from being taken outside and burned.

No one had *ever* seen anything like this before. There were long histories of diseases decimating African villages deep in the jungle. Some were given names by scientists, and others just came and went so fast that only the stories of the villagers cast any light on what the culprit of the decimation could be. Usually, a disease takes time to mutate. But with this it was as though it had begun making replicas of itself as it jumped from one host to another.

The villagers were bringing in their sick and dying, screaming *kindoki, kindoki.* Trying to get their sick to *anywhere* beyond their villages, to pass them off and try to run away. The unwell, who had become not themselves, now were believingly being poisoned by witchcraft. Guérisseurs had tried with their prayer and potions to cure the sick, but they could not. The jungle was hungry, devouring, relentless. Those infected by the dark magic of the bush devil must be cast out of the village before what had befallen one would befall them all.

As Isabella thought back, she remembered stories of the notary, *de Mussis,* describing how the Mongol army hurled plague-infected cadavers over the walls of the Crimean city of Caffa to create terror and hoping this would stop the 'mire of manifold weakness...' As the populace believed that the plague was the result of the *limitless capacity for evil...* the entire human race was being punished for no longer fearing the judgment of God. The doctors of the time wearing masks with long bird-like beaks, filled with perfumes and fragrant herbs, trying to purify the air. Clearly neither tossing the evil ridden corpses over the walls of Caffa or scenting the stench of the liquified rotted bodies made any difference. That plague killed around 200 million people.

But *it* never made sense. When Isabella was in medical school and residency she was taught that the plague was caused by *Yersinia*

*Pestis* and that fleas riding on the backs of rats were the culprit of the spread. Never, in the history of medicine, had there been *any* bacterium that had been able to gain a foothold and spread with that kind of ferocity *and* with that kind of killing power. If you got the plague—you died. From all the accounts of the Black Plague, the symptoms and how people died, it behaved more like a virus would. And now with this outbreak...

The question was not only what was causing this devastation but was there a way to contain it to these villages and could it be treated. One way that outbreaks of viruses in the past had been treated was by quarantining the villages with the military and letting those who were infected die off, treating their horrendous symptoms as best they could, but not allowing them outside of the perimeters of the village to spread whatever the hell *it* was. But this thing *had* spread beyond whatever village it had come from. As far as anyone knew no cases had shown up in any large population centers.

When the infected were brought into the hospital compound, those who brought them in were ordered to chain the infected's feet. They knew the *infected*, now only called that, were going to die. Even the Priest praying for the souls of the dying had lost all faith that Jesus would touch at least *one* of the suffering, perhaps a child, and spare them. But no such miracle was to be. Isabella thought that maybe God Himself was afraid of touching the infected ones.

Once the infected's feet were bound, the other end of the chain was hooked around hitching rails, cobbled together from old, galvanized pipes. Then when they died, men wearing masks and rubber gloves unhitched the chain of the dead, dragged them from their cot and pulled them into a pit with the other villagers that had died that day. They were then doused in petrol and set ablaze. Good Christ, the stench was retching.

What those who carried the dying in from the villages did not know was that they too were now infected and could not be allowed to leave what may be called a hospital, but really was no more than a camouflaged morgue. Those who brought the sick in on their backs, put them on a cot, and thinking they would go back to their villages, were told at gun point to go to the next tent, until they too inescapably began to show signs that death's scythe had come for them. If they refused, the government ordered they were to be shot. Isabella thought if she were one of the villagers, she would run just *to* get shot.

As she watched the horror, Isabella thought back to growing up in Paintsville. What she saw in her parents' clinic growing up had helped steel her for what she had to endure here. But even with the horrors of the black lung and the other queer calamities she'd witnessed, the outbreak that had exploded here was like some ungodly apparition that had come straight up from hell.

Isabella was sent here to try and discover what this *thing* was and where it had come from. She was not here as a physician to treat anyone as there was nothing to do except watch. In the past when an outbreak of hemorrhagic fevers had happened there had been one or two villages within close proximity, so it was easier to isolate where the origin of the infection had come from. But with this new outbreak, villagers were bringing in their infected from far and wide.

Fruit bats, rodents, fleas and ticks or macaques were the usual suspects, dank caves, trees, or the depth of the rainforests, harboring the deadliest viruses known to man. This too could be spread by bat guano, but it had to get to the bat as a vector and... how did it do that? But clearly first, *it* had to be discovered what the *it* was. The villagers kill and dry bats under breadfruit trees and then either eat it, after it has lost its moisture from baking in the sun or use it in making bat soup.

# Chapter 2

IN THE REMOTE PARTS of West Africa there was no good time to travel. It was always hot and often rainy, especially once you entered the jungle. The military would take Isabella anywhere she wanted to go. But... they were always cautious of guerillas or some faction that wanted to either rape or steal whatever you had. She had been here long enough that she knew some of the soldiers. They took good care of her and as best they could, kept her out of harm's way. This particular morning, she and two soldiers were making their way to one of the villages where many of the infected had come from.

The vehicle was so old and rusted that it lost parts off of this or that with each rut the driver couldn't negotiate around. Isabella had fallen asleep, leaning against the door, which had been tied shut, cracking open just enough to cause a spray of road dust to cover the side of her cheek and her bare shoulder. When they came up from a muddy gully the truck spun left, swinging the rear end around, causing the driver to come to a quick stop. Isabella said she had to pee. As she started to untie the door, one of the soldiers grabbed her shoulder, pulled his pistol and whispering said, "Don't move..." nodding for her to look to the flimsy floor. There coiled up was a carpet viper. "Christ..." she said under her breath. Maybe on *this* occasion actually meaning it as a prayer... The soldier slowly reached over her legs, and pulling her as close to him as possible, raised his pistol and fired three .45 rounds into the sleeping snake's head. The viper began spasmodically uncoiling and recoiling. Most of its head was gone but the rest of its body was whipping this way and that.

The soldier quickly pulled Isabella out onto the ground and shot the snake again. He knew that vipers can still be deadly even hours after they are killed. The other soldier got a rake that was in the back of the truck and hooked the tines around what was left of the viper, and pulled it out of the truck, onto the ground a safe distance away. The soldier who had pulled Isabella from the truck leaned down to make sure she was okay. Other than being covered in road dust, she was certainly better than she would have been if the viper had awakened and decided to strike. They figured it must have crawled in the truck that night, maybe even feeding on a cane rat, as they were always making a nest under the seats.

Isabella dropped her pants, squatted, and peed, and after, she shook herself and pulled her pants back up. They were on their way again. It was odd she thought that a snake had briefly interrupted their journey, remembering the words from Matthew: "*You snakes! You brood of vipers! How will you escape being condemned to hell?*" For a moment she thought that maybe the *condemned brood of vipers* had returned from the Nether region and brought whatever this goddamn virus was with them.

# Chapter 3

As they began encroaching on the first village, the forest began to fill with Green Monkeys. It was odd, Isabella thought, that the monks were silent. Usually, their deafening howling and cackling cause the hawk beak Pepper Birds to take flight by the thousands. But today it was as though they did not want to leave the safety of their perches. As they drove on, Isabella's eyes became lidded with suspicion as she and the soldiers began to see the road littered with dead monkeys. Hundreds were laying swollen, bloated and bleeding, just like the infected. Isabella yelled for the driver to stop so as not to run over the corpses for fear of releasing into the air whatever the monkeys died from. She also told the soldiers to put on their masks, goggles, rubber gloves and rubber boots. There were dead monkeys as far as they could see. It wasn't much longer to make the first village so they decided it would be best to go the rest of the way on foot. At least they could step over the corpses of the monks. Isabella also told one of the soldiers to radio back and have men bring flame throwers to incinerate the carcasses.

They had to be careful to step over the dead sabaeus as they traversed their way, using a machete to cut through brush that had grown over the little used road. When they approached the village, again Isabella was overcome with the silence. Only the occasional trill of the blue turaco interrupted the deafening quiet. When the village was within view, they saw bodies, like the monkeys, that littered the ground. Some of the villagers who lay at the outskirts looked like they had died while running away, as though they were being chased by a demon, as one of the soldiers said. Deeper into the heart of the village, bodies had been stacked one on top of the other and set on fire.

In one of the thatched huts the sound of moaning was coming through the hardened mud wall. As they entered the hut a woman, bleeding from her eyes and sitting in her own bloody waste, was holding a dead bloated infant to her breast. "Jesus Christ," Isabella said under her breath. One of the soldiers looked at Isabella and without speaking a word walked behind the clearly dying villager, pulled his .45, and shot the woman through the back of the head. Isabella witnessed the solider killing the villager without flinching. "Jesus, the rest of the world is sanitized from the ugliness of death," she thought, "and how people live behind imagined castle walls."

What was happening was akin to a nightmare. Even though blood samples had been sent back for analysis, the results had come back "inconclusive." But, they knew for sure, it was one hundred percent fatal. Even though they had tried to treat it early on, nothing had remotely halted or even slowed the deadly progression of the disease. Isabella knew that the most humane way of dealing with the virus was once someone was infected was to kill them. She didn't call it *euthanasia*, which Isabella considered a euphemism, it was what it is, killing another human being. But in this case, it was also the only merciful thing to do.

The soldiers had brought cans of petrol with them. They spent hours mounding the bodies into a pyre, dousing them with kerosine and setting them ablaze. Isabella took a blood sample from the villager the soldier had just shot to use as a baseline for the progression of the virus. The villager's blood would be hot with the virus in its most virulent form. She hoped when she sent it off that they would be able to begin to get an idea of how it killed so quickly, even *if* they couldn't identify what the virus was.

Once someone was infected there was no stopping its devolution to death. The only way of intervening was likely a vaccine, to stop it from being transmitted, which meant isolating each and every victim and letting the virus run its course and *then* to find where the hell it had come from. Once a vaccine was found, then it would be time to inoculate the villagers surrounding the area where the virus had emerged. They had not yet discovered what the circle of death was that the virus had made.

As they made their way back to the truck, Isabella knew this was just the beginning of what could become a viral apocalypse. Even though she had contacted the CDC, they were slow in responding, and much of the discussion, rather than centering on the identification of the disease, centered on 'what ifs...' "What if announcing what was occurring caused widespread panic," "This is an election year, and after all it *is* occurring in *Africa*..." "What if this was something those people brought about themselves and we've gone and raised a concern that just doesn't warrant it..." "What if..."

It was exhausting attempting to move beyond the bullshit of life-time administrators and then work directly with other scientists. But, in this situation, even working with other infectious disease experts, there was conflict and confusion. This damn thing behaved partly like a hemorrhagic fever. But the rapidity which it went from infection to death was unprecedented. Plus, in looking at it under an electron microscope, it didn't even resemble the Marburg virus, with its duck-like head protruding from a stick with a twist. But the Marburg duck head was oddly misshapen. The pathology made no sense.

They made their way to a half-dozen remote villages. All of them were decimated. Bloated Green Monkeys littering the jungle floor told them they were nearing a village. As they approached what they hoped was the last village, a monk bleeding from its eyes fell from the trees and crashed into the window of the truck, causing the driver to swerve, slam on the brakes, pull his .45, and shoot through the cracked, spidered windshield. When it was hit by the gun shot the billowed monkey seemed to explode in an array of wet tenderloin, covering the windshield. Isabella screamed, "Hold your breath!" and then opened the door and threw herself onto the ground with the soldiers following. They crawled toward the back of the truck away from the corpuscled debris of the monkey. As they made their way beyond the truck, the soldiers did exactly what Isabella had taught them.

When Isabella was back in Paintsville, she always carried a knife. Everyone did. It wasn't a weapon; it was just part of what you put in your pocket every morning. You could never tell when you needed to skin a fish or cut a piece of rope, everyone would say. Daddies and mommas carried one at work and boys and girls carried one in their britches at school. Even Isabella's mother and father, both being doctors, carried a pocketknife. She remembered Moses, her father, saying how many times he'd needed his knife to do an emergency tracheotomy when he'd been out somewhere without his medical bag.

God help any youngin', as she fondly remembered children being called, who would dare to pull out a knife if they were in fact fighting. By God, if they didn't get their ass whipped in the fight, they'd sure enough get their ass tanned either by their teacher or their mommas and daddies when they got home.

When they got a safe distance to stand up, Isabella pulled the knife from the sheath around her waist, after putting on a pair of surgical gloves she kept in her pocket. One of the soldiers walked toward her, turned his back to her while she cut off his fatigues. She did the same to the other soldier. Cutting them in such a way that they fell to the ground, and she didn't have to touch them. Then one of the soldiers put on a pair of latex gloves and cut her clothes off. They tossed the gloves onto the pile of clothes and walked away. It had taken her a while to be comfortable with being naked or relieving herself in public places, especially around the soldiers. But it was different here. At times your life could depend on what you had on or didn't and being self-conscious or reluctant could have dire consequences. If any of the virus had splattered on them this could be one of those times. There was a duffle bag in the back of the truck that one of the soldiers grabbed as they were getting clear. In it was a complete change of clothes, should something unexpected happen.

Walking as fast as they could, one of the soldiers radioed that they needed assistance and to send another truck to retrieve them. Isabella took one of the soldier's pistols and emptied the clip into the gas tank of the truck until it ignited and exploded, throwing a swell of flame high into the air.

"Jesus Christ this is a war zone," she said. It would take hours for a patrol to pick them up. And who, other than to the army, were they going to report what they'd found?

Isabella had been called to investigate the cause of a "small outbreak" in Liberia. "It doesn't look like much," they said at the CDC, but they wanted to get whatever it was shut down before it got out of hand and caused "unnecessary concern." In addition to the blood samples, she had also taken photographs of the condition of the bodies, both dead and dying.

One of the soldiers said to Isabella that when he shot the monkey that the round shattered the glass with such a force that it likely blew any air borne particles away from them and not toward them. They felt as protected as they could, under the circumstances. Especially with them throwing themselves out of the truck so quickly and then incinerating it. The fireball that resulted from Isabella shooting the petrol tank should have killed any virus that had escaped from the monkey's tissues.

They had gone well beyond where they encountered the monkey carcasses on the road. So, she figured that the virus must have a radius of exposure. In fact, it was like seeing a snow line when looking up into the mountains. There was a definitive line of demarcation. If they could get an idea of how large the circumference was, they could at least begin to figure out what villages were in that circle. Any tribes that were in that circle of exposure were already or soon would be dead. The army would have to come in and burn that area of the jungle. Once they were picked up, she would have them take a spotter chopper so they could identify the area. It would not be hard to do as there would be bodies of both the villagers and monkeys strewn about.

The biggest two worries now were where had the goddamn virus had come from and how far had it spread beyond the villages. The villagers who had been brought into the hospital compound would have spread debris, one way or another in the jungle along the way. They would also have to determine how long it could live outside of a host, and what kind of host the virus seeks out to replicate itself.

# Chapter 4

IT WAS SEVERAL HOURS before Isabella and the two soldiers were
picked up and taken back to the make-shift hospital compound. In
a few hours an army medivac chopper had picked up Isabella and
began doing concentric circle runs, starting with the first village and
working out from there. As they began to open the circle, it became
clear that the area of decimation was larger than she had thought.
There was the center of a village with bodies spread everywhere. It
seemed that the dying villagers even had laid on top of each other in
their desperation and died where they had collapsed. The number of
bodies dissipated as they got further to the edge of the village. Then
the bodies fell off in numbers and the dead monkeys increased. Isabella
had an image of hundreds of Green Monkeys encircling the village,
few daring to enter, watching the villagers die and then those monks
who had plucked up what they imagined to be courage returned to
infect those who chose not to waste their fearlessness on foolishness.
She leaned against the chopper's jump seat and felt the whirl of the
wind from the chopper blades blow through the evac doors as she
saw the bloated bodies of the villagers.

As they approached what they hoped was the last village that lay
at the far end of the circle of death, she suddenly screamed into the
spit mike for the chopper pilot to come back around, tighten his turn
and drop down closer. The pilot began to emphatically say that he
would not, "*Kindoki, kindoki...*" Isabella heard in her headset. She
reached over the seat, put her hand on his shoulder and waved for
him to reduce their altitude. Reluctantly he changed the pitch of
the blades and Isabella could see the earth begin to get closer to the
chopper. She then told him to hover while she leaned out the evac

door and began to scan the village below. "There..." the pilot heard her yell into his ear as he looked back and saw her finger pointing down toward the village.

She looked to be about five or six. She only wore sandals and what looked like an amulet necklace that hung around her neck. The child was going from one pile of bodies to another. As best she could tell, Isabella thought she looked hysterical. Isabella told the pilot to put the chopper down. This time he was more adamant that he was not going to land the helicopter. Then he heard in his ear, "Bring this fucking chopper down or I'll jump out the goddamn door!" He looked back at Isabella, shaking his head. As the pilot began to tap the collective down, Isabella began to gown up and ask herself why the little girl wasn't dead. The bodies were clearly rotting in the dense forest. She was surprised the leopards had not already begun scavenging. Which of course would disperse the virus even more.

When they got about six feet above the ground, the pilot said for Isabella to keep her head down, out of way of the rotors, as she stepped out onto the landing strut and jumped. He said to signal when she wanted to be picked up. Isabella hit harder than she would have thought for only jumping about six feet, but the down draft from the blades was pushing her into the ground. In but a brief second the chopper was airborne again. Isabella began making her way through the piles of corpses, looking for the child. Then peering out from one of the huts she saw her. She was sure she looked like a monster to the child, gowned up the way she was. But, to her astonishment, the little girl came running towards her. She frantically began waving her hands and pointing to the bodies screaming, "*Lée Núu*..." Having been in Liberia now for a while, Isabella knew this was *Kpelle* for *mother*...

There was no way of identifying any of the bodies, given the bloating, not to mention many of the corpses had exploded from the thick heat and massive hemorrhages. Isabella pulled the child close attempting as best she could to comfort her. In looking at her there was no indication that she was ill with the virus. She was, besides being terrified, exhibiting no obvious signs of hemorrhages. Isabella had noticed a small stream running through the jungle not far from the village. She took the little girl and made their way to the stream. She sat the child down in the water and began bathing her, taking fern leaves, and using them as one might use bamboo to exfoliate and sluff off old skin. She reached into her rucksack and took out another anticontamination suit and indicated she wanted to put it on the little girl. Isabella continued to think that the child would at any time begin resisting or even attempt to run away. But she didn't. The suit swallowed the girl, but Isabella tied the arms and legs up so she could at least walk and not be bound above the waist like being in a strait jacket. Then she put a mask over the child's nose and mouth. Once they had made their way back to the center of the village, she signaled for the chopper to pick them up.

# Chapter 5

ISABELLA STOOD AT THE center of the village, surrounded by bodies, signaling with her hand for the chopper to descend. She could see the hesitation in the pilot in the slowness of his response to her hand signals. Finally, she made as strong of a downward motion for him to land as she knew before the bottom of the chopper could be seen descending. With the chopper hovering barely above the ground, she lifted the little girl into the back of the chopper and then climbed in after her. The child clung to Isabella as she strapped them in. As the seat belts were clicking secure the pilot began to rapidly ascend.

In a short while they were putting down on the outskirts of the makeshift hospital compound. Isabella took the child to one of the tents where she could examine her. She carefully took off the gown and began to look for any signs that she had been infected. There was no telltale mask like ghosting that Isabella had seen in other patients. Yet, although the child may not be exhibiting signs of the disease, she certainly could be a carrier. But the other possibilities was that somehow she had a natural immunity or had not had close enough proximity to someone who was infected. Isabella took a blood draw and cultured the inside of her mouth. It was odd, but the child offered no more resistance now than when Isabella rescued her from the village. She wasn't docile, rather she seemed to have an understanding that Isabella was trying to help her.

Isabella stayed with the little girl throughout the night, both getting up several times to relieve themselves. The next morning Isabella went to the blood analyzer, expecting to see devastating numbers, thinking that the virus had just not caught up to her yet. But her blood values were exactly where they should be for a little girl of her age. It would take a week or so for the culture to grow anything, if, in fact, there was anything besides normal flora present. Until then, unless she was in the field or watching other patients die, Isabella would remain by her side. The question, haunting her, was why wasn't the child ill.

As the days went on Isabella continued to check the culture for any signs that something out of the ordinary was growing. But on the seventh day nothing was there. For a week now, Isabella had rarely left the child's side. She had bathed her, took her to the toilet, and fed her. The little girl sat and waited with Isabella. That morning and before the little girl awoke, Isabella made her way to the lab area to check the petri dish. *Nothing, nothing* but normal flora.

She came back to where she and the child had been sleeping. In this week Isabella had learned the little girl's name was *Chidinma*. The local woman also said the name Chidinma was Nigerian and meant something like, *God is Beautiful*. The woman told Chidinma that the woman who was tending to her was named *Isabella*.

Isabella roused Chidinma. As Chidinma sat up Isabella began to unzip her protective gown. For the first time in what was a very long week Chidinma took in a breath of unfiltered air. Then Isabella showed Chidinma how to unzip her suit. Once they had disposed of their gowns, Isabella and Chidinma washed under an improvised shower, basically a body bag, filled with water and piped out through a rubber hose. The woman who had brought them food and water asked if she should notify the local authorities about Chidinma and have her taken to a temporary home for children whose parents have been killed. "No," Isabella said, "That won't be necessary..."

# Chapter 6

IT WAS GOING TO be a wildfire operation. It was a little-known critical operation that most governments had in place, should a viral or bacterial entity ever get out of control within a geographically defined and containable space. There are never any records kept of any of the operations. The only thing that is logged are the specific clinical effects of the entity and since it was a wildfire operation, it was assumed to have a kill factor of 100% and unstoppable by any other means. Even the viral or bacterial entity was never given a name, only a number, in this case it was labeled 666. She hated the cliche, but... it seemed right. The virus from Hell.

Isabella and a group of soldiers had mapped out a series of concentric circles. The farthest circle indicated a neutral zone. One in which there had been no indications of the virus and then moving inward to what was designated the hot zone. Everything contained within the concentric circles would be incinerated. The problem was, that villagers further out in the circle would die. Warnings were made but... It was a wretched option and for some would be untenable. But there was also nothing Isabella could do, and pragmatically, it had to be stopped.

It was not long after the sun had come up when the area that had been mapped out by the military was immolated. An aerial ignition device was dropped from four different helicopters, all hovering at equal points. Blocks of gelled petrol were designed to ignite when white phosphorous detonators broke open on impact. As Isabella watched from the lead chopper, she remembered white phosphorous was called the *devils element*, for being so unstable and volatile. Not to mention it being the *13th* element to be discovered. How fitting white phosphorous was the catalyst to set off the eradication of virus *666*.

When the devices were dropped, the choppers ascended rapidly and rotated to the right, tilting the blades, so the incineration would be forced toward the inner ring. Ground crews after the drop had come to extinguish any flames that may begin moving beyond the outer perimeters. They were well into the dry season and there had been a high evaporation rate of the soil, which made it both ideal and risky.

As they observed from now high above the inferno, everything was being decimated. Isabella believed she had determined how far out they needed to go to account for fleeing monkeys trying like hell to escape the fire moving for them. But... she thought they had, as best they could, calculated a line of demarcation, where no dying monkeys had been observed and then worked their way back to the hot zones. It had potentially perilous consequences but so did doing nothing and waiting for whatever the virus was to burn itself out or of course, much worse, spread beyond the area and encampment. They should be able to determine in a few weeks if they had been successful in quelling the outbreak.

Two weeks had gone by now and the cases coming in had dwindled down, until the last few days when there were none presenting. Isabella and the military commander put together a group that would go back into the burned-out region to survey the destruction and to bury the bodies from the destroyed villages. Soldiers were also assigned to bulldoze under as many of the monkeys as they could find. Isabella would take samples from the villagers and the monks to see if there was any sign of the virus.

It became increasing more desolate as they made their way from the outer edge of the burn to the center. The closer they got to the villages, corpses of incinerated green monkeys littered the blackened forest floor. Isabella took tissue samples from several monkeys, noting the distance from the center of the village. Once they came to the perimeter of the village's they saw bodies lying about that had been carbonized by the intensity of the fire. Most of the skin had been burned away and fragments of skeletonized bones remained. She couldn't imagine any virus particle surviving this kind of heat, but as much as she could, Isabella took tissue samples from the core of the spinal columns of the dead villagers. It was a horrific scene, one that, unless you were trained to even imagine it, would never be believed. What was once vibrant villages were now nothing more than remnants of ash and bones. Isabella thought it looked like what was left of an archeological unearthing.

# Chapter 7

ISABELLA AND CHIDINMA RETURNED to Atlanta a few months after the outbreak had abated. But the lag time in leaving was waiting until immigration and the authorities had cleared the way for Isabella to adopt Chidinma. The child was left with nothing, her parents were not only dead they had been incinerated when her village was burned. She couldn't even go back to identify their bodies. Chidinma would have gone to an orphanage where, in this part of Africa, there were thousands of children, who for the most part, were lost in the morass of disorganization and chaos that thrived in western Africa.

Isabella had never yearned to have children and found in her work what she considered a calling that was stronger than a desire to create a family. Yet when she and Chidinma first met under such horrendous circumstances, a knowing came to Isabella that their lives had become inseparably intertwined. With Isabella white as snow and Chidinma black as night, they would go through life together as mother and daughter.

It was surprising to Isabella that Chidinma didn't seem to have much trepidation about coming to America and with beginning to fit into a profoundly new way of existing. She had gone from being in an isolated village in Africa to Atlanta, Georgia. Her adaption Isabella thought was one borne out of curiosity rather than fear and anxiety. She also had shown herself to have a natural ability to learn new languages. Shortly after they met, Isabella discovered Chidinma's linguistic gifts. It wasn't long until they were able to communicate in full sentences. When they left Liberia, Isabella took all of the blood samples that she had pulled from Chidinma when she was watching for any signs of the 666 Virus to emerge. Once she got back to the

CDC, Isabella froze the samples in her lab. After she returned, Isabella was promoted to the Chief of The Viral Special Pathogens Branch (VSPB) for the work that she had done in Africa. Not to mention that there were few virologists who had the experience or understanding about the structure and behavior of the more exotic viruses.

One of the first things she did when she was made branch chief was to conduct and in-house seminar on what had transpired in Liberia. It was interesting how many of the other scientists confronted her with their disbelief of how quickly the 666 Virus could go from initial infection to death. As she herself had said many times, "...nothing like it had ever been seen before." The speed of cellular liquification was unheard of by any known virus. They didn't know where it came from, how the host became infected, and most importantly, how it killed. Isabella could only identify the symptom progression. As a matter of fact, the only initial symptoms were severe diarrhea and an emerging fever. If someone came into an ER the likelihood would be that they would be diagnosed with amoebic dysentery or food poisoning, especially with the way physicians were being trained these days. So much of the time she saw doctors coming out of residencies with a profound lack of curiosity and willingly falling into what she had begun to call *production medicine*. In seeking employment, the first consideration was on-call time and the number of days off every month. Some hospitals were now even beginning to call patients, customers. Hospitals were even giving physicians bonuses based upon how quickly they got patients in and out of their office or the ER. Private practices were being consumed by hospital corporations and doctors were called *physician partners*. Bonuses and incentives were littered throughout the partnering contract agreements but sorely lacking was even one mention of patient care. Isabella told her colleagues that if she ever met another doctor who called their patients *customers* they would have to come and bail her out of jail after being charged with assault.

# Chapter 8

DR. CHARLES LAPIDES HELD MANY beliefs that made him challenging for his colleagues. He believed that the sick and infirmed came to *him* after being inflicted with whatever malady God had chosen to give them, to wreak havoc on their bodies and spirits. It was Dr. Lapides' *call* not only to cure them of their physical ills but also to save their wretched souls. As you entered his office a plaque on the wall read, *"A war erupted in Heaven in which the Archangel Michael and his angels fought against Satan and his angels (Revelations 12:7-9). Satan and the other fallen angels were defeated and as a punishment for their rebellion they were cast out of Heaven (Revelations 12:9, Luke 10:18). Satan became the Prince of Demons (Matthew 12:24) and he and the other fallen angels were hurled to the earth (Revelations 12:9) and ultimately condemned to Hell (Matthew 25:41)." God has chosen to anoint me with His salt and light to bless my patients."* The doc hadn't been successful as a medical student and he would never say where he had graduated amongst his other classmates. His professors, he would say, had been against him all the way through, especially when he would confront them for their idolatry and *preaching* anti-biblical ways. The Lord's medicine was *prayer* and in order to avoid medical school becoming dangerous to one's faithfulness, you had to be true to your devotional life above all else.

Dr. Lapides' office was in Wilton, North Dakota. Folks up that way called Wilton a passthrough when heading up north to Canada, and the townspeople were known for being just about as friendly as friendly could be. They said that no one in Wilton would ever go hungry because once it was found out that you were not being fed properly, they'd get enough food together to take care of your hunger for a month of Sundays. All in all, though, there wasn't much to it and the trains that had once been so prominent a part of its landscape had stopped running long ago. Now, a bus or two a week made a drop-off and a pick-up for the few who needed a ride to here and there.

Most of Wilton tolerated having Dr. Lapides as the only doc in town. It wouldn't do them any good if they didn't. There were some though who went to him just to have their souls cleaned out. A couple of smart-alecks said that Dr. Lapides did holy high-colonics. For the most part, though, Dr. Lapides wanted to prescribe just as few medicines as he could get by with and treat rheumatism that the old ladies came in and incessantly complained about. It was a Thursday when a man of average height got off the last bus until Tuesday the next week. He mumbled to the bus driver, who was glad to get rid of him, wanting to know where he could find a doctor in town. The mumbling man stumbled his way down the block until he came to a white frame house with a shingle hung out front. In front of the house was a leaning post, pushing up out of the wet, spongy soil of the last spring rains. The sign read, *Charles Lapides, M.D., General Practice*. Before the man swung open the office door and collapsed onto the floor, he looked up into the sky and saw a sparrow ascending straight up in the air like a soul departing. The last thing he would see were the hundreds of angel figurines scattered throughout the waiting room and an old theater organ set in the corner, with a full panel of pull stops to the right and left of the three manuals. At that moment, right before he died, the man thought he had opened the door to the sanctum of Heaven.

As the bus approached Wilton, the man had kept getting sicker and sicker. He had gotten on in Fargo, carrying only a small bundle tied up in twine. He'd looked feverish, cheeks flushed and had dried blood around his lips and eyes. How he had come to Fargo was a question. He never stopped rambling on about this and that, none of which made any sense. The only thing the young girl who was sitting beside him was able to make out was something about how he had tried to hide from Satan but was found and defiled and was now decaying. "Get away, get away..." he screamed in a strange accent to the girl. At one point the bus driver told him to go sit in the back and keep his mouth shut. By the time the bus arrived in Wilton, bloody piss was running down his legs. His filthy canvas shoes made a sloshing sound as he walked up the center aisle toward the rear of the bus, looking for a vacant seat along the way.

The receptionist, leaving for the day out the side door, saw the man collapse and yelled for Dr. Lapides to immediately come to the waiting room. In but a few short steps the doctor had rolled the man onto his back, convinced that he must have been stabbed or shot from all the blood under his body. As he began pulling his clothes aside, he saw massive exuding purplish welts covering his chest. The man's head lolled to one side, when a huge bolus of bloody vomit came erupting from his mouth. "My Lord, my God..." Dr. Lapides thought to himself, "how could this be?" To which he immediately began praying, believing that he was encountering the beginning of the end times. He didn't attempt to do anything to resuscitate the man, whose heart had stopped right after he vomited. Dr. Lapides suddenly found himself consumed by a sense of Holy contemplation. He righted himself to an erect of a state as he had ever been. Thinking that he wanted to make sure the Lord saw him respectfully standing at attention, walked over to the organ, pushing the sound peddle to the floor, as his fingers began playing, *How Great Thou Art...* As he played, the organ's keys became soiled with the blood of the dead man that had coated Dr. Lapides hands when he rolled him over.

# Chapter 9

ISABELLA HATED ATLANTA. SHE often said that people in the United States would be a hell of a lot healthier if they could just pee outside. Americans are so obsessed with cleanliness, she thought that they were killing themselves. She knew it was being ridiculous, but since becoming the Chief of the VSPB she found herself consumed by bureaucrats wanting indented explanations with childlike drawings showing how viruses come into being and replicate. Then they spent most of their time calculating how a certain virus could hurt or even help their reelection chances. "Jesus!" she would adamantly say as she left each meeting.

When they first returned from Africa, Isabella enrolled Chidinma in a private school. One that would help her acquire the basic knowledge for her age. What she hadn't expected was how quickly Chidinma had excelled and surpassed her grade level. It wasn't long that Isabella had her tested and found that her I.Q. was well into the gifted range.

# Chapter 10

DR. LAPIDES CALLED THE SHERIFF and told him he had a dead man in his waiting room, and he thought he should come over and take possession of the body.

A sheriff of a small town surprisingly sees a lot of dead bodies. Hell, some old people drop dead eating a meal with their family. There was one fella who was having the same argument that he'd been having with his wife of fifty years, day in and day out. Until that final day being right when he was just opening his mouth to shout what he'd always shouted, that he grabbed his chest and fell face down, dead as dead could be, right into his bowl of mashed potatoes.

The sheriff got called by a neighbor lady who'd just happened to bring a pie over from next door, right when old Edgar dropped dead. The neighbor lady, looking at Edgar laying there dead, thought that if he hadn't died from a heart attack, he'd of sure smothered to death with his whole head buried in that bowl of buttered up mashed potatoes. Edgar's wife though just went on bickering, now with no one there to ever again say anything back, not so much as realizing that he wasn't ever going to be lifting his potato covered face out of that bowl.

When the sheriff got to Dr. Lapides' office, he wasn't sure what he was even seeing. It was like someone had turned on a spigot of blood and let it run all over Dr. Lapides waiting room. It looked more like a murder scene. Dr. Lapides told the sheriff that the man had just turned up in his waiting room, right when he was closing his office for the day. Then he fell over dead and started bleeding out. "I've never seen him before, he just turned up here..." The sheriff asked Dr. Lapides if he had any idea what the hell the man had died of. He said he hadn't but, "In the name of Jesus... I believe we are looking at the end times... This is nothing like I have ever even imagined seeing. When I rolled him over blood was coming out of his eyes with such pressure that it sprayed me in the face. I tried to wipe it off as best I could, but this man was bleeding from places that a human isn't supposed to bleed from." The sheriff began to lean down to check the pockets of the deceased. And at that moment Dr. Lapides had enough good sense to scream at the sheriff and wave him back away from the body. "Don't touch him. I think it's too late for me, but I don't want it to be too late for you too." The sheriff said he had been on patrol all day and hadn't seen any new cars coming or going off the main road. "Just the bus," he said, "It's gotta be the bus."

The bus driver, who made driving a bus seem like he was the captain of an air liner, had never been seen dressed in anything other than his uniform, starched shirt, service cap and tight neck cinched black-watch-tie with tiny busses embroidered on it. He always stopped about halfway between Wilton and Washburn to have a cigarette or two and to let it be known to any ruffians who might be causing a ruckus that the Painted Wood Crick fishing pullout was where they'd be walking from. Joe, known to those who made the run regularly, knew him to be a man of no nonsense and if need be, he could be mean as a snake. On this particular day, Joe had a local boy who'd gotten on there in Wilton. That sonofabitch hadn't wasted any time before he began hurling untoward comments to a couple of Mennonite ladies who were headed up north to join the weekend encircling prayer. Wanting to bring the Lord's attention and all to the Paganism that was taking over the world. Joe, looking back in his mirror, saw that boy reach over his seat and pull the haube off one of the prayful ladies. Joe himself wasn't particularly a believer of much of anything but he sure as hell did believe most fervently that folks had the right to believe whatever they wanted, as long as they didn't try and force it on someone else. And these ladies were about as devout as could be and sure enough kept to themselves. When Joe turned the bus into the Painted Wood Crick pullout, he didn't even bother to have his cigarette before he marched down the aisle, took that hoodlum by his ear, twisted the hell out of it and dragged him toward the door. Then Joe turned that boy's scrawny ass in the air and kicked him right out the folding bus doors. When that little bastard hit the ground, he thought he'd been kicked by a mule. As soon as he got to his feet, he went running like a cat who'd had turpentine poured up its ass. Joe went over, stood by the crick, lit his first cigarette, and waved for the passengers to get off the bus and stretch their legs. A few of the passengers were starting to sweat and feel weak in the knees.

As Joe stood there smoking, he saw the boy he'd tossed from the bus, downstream a bit, bent over the crick splashing water onto his face. Then the boy just rolled over and seemed to fall asleep. Joe flipped his cigarette in the air and mumbled "Good riddance."

## Chapter 11

Dr. Lapides was told by the sheriff to stay in his office and lock his doors. Thinking he'd just seen the worst thing he hoped to never see again, the sheriff ran out of the office and jumped in his patrol car. He may be able to reach the afternoon bus before it reached Washburn, he said out loud to no one, as he sped down the main street to where it intersected with Highway 83. Turning north he flipped on his lights and moved the needle of the speedometer to a wavering 90. Washburn was only about twenty minutes or so up the road and he knew the bus driver always stopped at the Painted Wood Crick pullout to have a cigarette. About ten miles out he could see the passengers starting to get back on the bus. The sheriff pulled his cruiser in front of the bus, keeping its lights on. He got out of the car as Joe began walking towards him. "Joe," he called, "...don't come any closer. Either get back on the bus or stay where you are."

Joe, not having any idea what was going on, yelled back, "What the hell is going on, Sheriff?"

"There's been an emergency Joe, stay back, do what I'm telling you..." Joe still was walking toward the sheriff, when he saw him pull his service revolver pointing it. "Do what I tell you, Joe, or I'll have to drop you." Joe, stopping in his tracks now, said he hadn't done anything wrong. Thinking that somehow, even though it didn't make any sense, that he was in trouble for throwing the good-for-nothing off the bus. "Joe, you ain't done *nothing* wrong, there's a medical emergency and I can't let you go any further up the road. You have to get back on the bus and stay there with the passengers until *I* can figure out what the hell is going on. I don't know how long this is going to take but you all can't get back off the bus. I know it's going to upset some folks, but you can't, you may all be contagious with something, I just don't know yet." Joe, not being happy about it, nonetheless said he would comply with the sheriff's orders and make sure the passengers stayed put. "You're in charge, Joe, I am officially deputizing you under North Dakota Special Occasions or Emergency Situations law. You hereby have the legal authorization to do whatever it takes to keep those folks on that bus."

The other question that was sticking in the sheriff's craw was where the man came from and how he'd gotten to Wilton in the first place. He was a real black Negro fella but given how folks go from here to there to just about anywhere, there was no telling how he'd gotten to Fargo to have boarded the bus in the first place. No one on the bus or the sheriff for that matter knew they had at best a few days to live.

# Chapter 12

IT HAD ONLY BEEN a few hours now and Dr. Lapides was feeling a fever coming on. It wasn't a great fever, just one that was beginning to warm him up. But even though he hadn't been first in his medical school class, he knew that it had to be connected to the fellow who'd just died a while ago in his waiting room. As a matter of fact, he was still waiting for whomever was going to pick up the corpse. Dispatch had notified the local funeral home to do a pick-up but they sure as hell were taking their time.

Just as Dr. Lapides frustration was getting the best of him and his fever was showing its presence on his brow, Flint and Sons Mortuary's hearse arrived. When the two men entered the waiting room and saw the dead man's swollen, contorted body lying on the floor in a pool of blood, they like the sheriff thought he had been murdered. As they leaned over him one of the men said, "What the hell are those black splotches all over his face?" Dr. Lapides said he didn't know. The man had just showed up at his office and died, right where he is. One of the men asked if they could catch anything from the body, Dr. Lapides looking puzzled himself, said he thought the man had something infectious, but he had no idea what it was, so it would probably be good if the men wore a mask and gloves while they were handling the body.

As the dieners were rolling the dead man onto a plastic tarp, a gurgling sound seemed to erupt from within his pants as globs of thick, viscous bloody liquid poured out his pants legs. Both men jumped back from the body, not just from the sudden eruption but also because of the stench that now filled the room. One of the men ran outside and vomited. When he came back inside, he yelled, "What the fuck was wrong with this guy?" Dr. Lapides, just wanting the corpse out of his waiting room, said he would help them and went back into his clinic and found some sheets to absorb the leaking liquids. After Dr. Lapides had packed the sheets around the corpse he said, "Now push the tarp up under him as far as you can get it..." One of the men leaned down and pushed the plastic under the man's shoulders, side, legs and feet. Afterwards, Dr. Lapides told the men to come to the other side of the man's body. Then the three of them stood at the dead man's head, side, and legs, and used their feet to roll him onto the tarp. When they got him over onto the plastic, they leaned down and pulled the tarp over him, then one of the men pulled the strings to cinch the covering. The two men dragged the man more than carry him to the waiting hearse, leaving a dripping, viscous trail.

As best they could the morgue assistants pulled the body up over the bumper of the hearse, ripping a hole in the tarp, causing the fluids that had pooled in the bottom to pour out onto the road. "Fuck..." one of the assistants said, "Let's get this guy back to the funeral home and be done with this."

Right after they had picked up the body, Dr. Lapides began vomiting. First the fluid was clear liquid. It wasn't long before it became bright red. He thought that even if he had contracted something from the dead man in his waiting room, that there is *no* virus in the world that moves this fast. "Hell..." he said out loud, "Even most poisons don't bring on symptoms this fast." But he thought that he should go on down to the ER in Bismarck.

It took about an hour from Wilton to get to the ER. Usually, it didn't take more than thirty minutes or so, but the further Dr. Lapides drove the more disoriented he became. He also had to stop several times to vomit along the side of the road. By the time he got to the hospital he was leaking bloody diarrhea. Swollen, sky black weals were starting to come to the surface of his skin. He somehow managed to make it to the double doors of the ER, thankful they opened by themselves. Then Dr. Lapides collapsed. The triage nurse called for assistance when she saw the man go down. She also saw the trail of blood showing his path to the ER doors. When she saw he was pooling blood underneath him and diaphoretic, the nurse immediately ruled out her initial thoughts of the man having been stabbed or shot. Now her thoughts were "infectious." And in that consideration, she screamed for everyone to clear the area and called for Dr. Conteh.

The moment Dr. Aniru Conteh came through the ER doors into the waiting area he stopped in his tracks. He stood frozen, staring at the man lying on the floor, now convulsing, bleeding profusely from his eyes, nose, and mouth. Likely he thought from his rectum and penis also. He hadn't seen anything like this since arriving in the United States from Sierra Leone.

Dr. Conteh was considered the world's foremost authority on Lassa Fever. He was doing a round of appointments at different hospitals in the United States as a way of educating other physicians on identifying hemorrhagic fevers. It was his second day in Bismarck after having been throughout the East and Midwest. After Bismarck he was to go onto Billings, Seattle and then to LA and then fly back to Sierra Leone. He had a feeling that he would be in Bismarck a while longer, never imagining he would ever see anything like *this* here.

Immediately Dr. Conteh called for an isolation gown, mask, and gloves. He also ordered security to take everyone who had been in the waiting area into an isolation room and further to lock down the hospital. The man lying on the floor was gasping and hyperventilating profusely. Dr. Conteh pulled a syringe of a Benzodiazepine, squeezed the man's jaws enough to get the syringe between his clinched teeth and under his tongue, then slowly he pushed the plunger until the barrel was empty. It was not possible to find a vein under these circumstances, plus it would be far too dangerous to any of the other medical personnel to have a needle anywhere near the man, that they could possibly be stuck with. Dr. Conteh stayed with the dying man, until his seizures slowed, and he began to calm, showing the effects of the medication. What hadn't been known to the other staff was that Dr. Conteh had given the man twice the dosage of the Benzo, knowing that he had to get some kind of response as soon as possible. And most importantly, no matter what was done, the man only had a short time to live. In about thirty minutes, the man's respirations had slowed to being barely perceptible. Then he gasped. His chest rising and falling for the last time. Dr. Conteh immediately put into place the isolation protocol. Within a few minutes two more staff gowned up came and took Dr. Lapides to the morgue for autopsy. In this case, Dr. Conteh would conduct the post himself. Before he attended to the patients and staff who had been in the admissions area when the man came in, he had a call to make.

# Chapter 13

Isabella had long finished for the day and was mulling this and that at the VSPB. The this and that was mostly about leaving the CDC. She had never envisioned her life being dominated by anything other than field work. And, on this day, Isabella had come to the decision that it was time to move. There were several universities who were making offers of an endowed professorship, now it was a matter of whittling the offers down to what would work best for her and Chidinma. That was when her pager told her she had a call waiting and with the three "***" after the number it indicated the call was urgent.

When she answered the phone she heard, "Hello, Dr. Kitchen, this is Dr. Aniru Conteh, perhaps from your work you may have heard of me." "Most certainly I am familiar with *your* work, especially your paper '*The Enigma of Virus 666 – The Virus That Shouldn't Be.*'"

"That is why I am calling."

"Hello Dr. Conteh, of course I am familiar with your work, it is *seminal* in how we now approach our understanding of hemorrhagic fevers, how can I help you?"

"Dr. Kitchen, I wish I was calling you under different circumstances, but... I believe the virus you wrote of has returned and broken free of its jungle confinement. If I am right, and if your understanding of the virus is correct, then I fear we are all in very deep trouble."

Dr. Conteh went on to tell Isabella about the man who died in the ER waiting room and now lay sealed in a cadaver bag in the morgue. After Dr. Conteh finished, the only thing Isabella could say was, "God help us..."

Isabella told Dr. Conteh that she would get a flight out to Bismarck.

She immediately contacted the base commander at Dobbins and informed him she had a possible Level 1 Public Health Emergency. She needed an immediate flight to Bismarck. She grabbed the emergency bag she kept in her office, called Chidinma and headed north to Dobbins.

The Base Guard Shack had been alerted a VIP would arrive shortly. APs would meet her and take her to the flight line where a C-130 would be fueled and already cleared for takeoff. A few hours later they touched down at Minot AFB. From there Isabella was shuffled to a helicopter. A half an hour later the chopper was putting down in a field across from the hospital.

The helicopter's struts steadied the chopper on the ground, the whirling props created a hurricane of dust. As Isabella unclasped her seat belt, she looked out the window and saw Dr. Conteh ducking his head from the rotating props as he ran toward the chopper through the stirred-up debris filled blur. When the rear airman slid the gun door back, Isabella saw the ominous gaze of Dr. Conteh come into view. As their eyes met for the first time, she didn't feel the down draft from the rotors as much as felt the foreboding presence of the *Sword of Damocles.*

"We have to do the post as soon as possible. I want to see what we have while he is fresh. He was decomping even while he was still alive. I have never even imagined anything like this."

Isabella nodded, fully understanding what he was saying.

# Chapter 14

DR. LAPIDES' BAGGED CORPSE lay on the autopsy table. Dr. Conteh and Dr. Kitchen, now gowned up, unzipped the body bag. They had the table tilted up about six degrees so the fluids could drain into a sealed collection bin, then, when they had finished, it would go directly into an incinerator. This was the first time Dr. Kitchen had done a post on a 666 cadaver. When she was in West Africa there were no facilities where it was safe to get a sighted view of what the virus did to the body. They didn't remove Dr. Lapides from the body bag. It was just unzipped enough to expose his torso. Dr. Kitchen did the initial Y cut, then Dr. Conteh sawed the ribs off and cut away the sternal plate so they could see the organs.

What they found was worse than Dr. Kitchen imagined. She had seen hundreds of deaths from the virus that she had encountered in Liberia, but the effect on the internal organs was devastating. They were for all practical purposes liquified. The liver, lungs and spleen were nothing more than structureless globs of a crimson mass. If they hadn't known where the organs came from anatomically, Dr. Kitchen and Dr. Conteh couldn't tell *what* they were. The heart fared slightly better because of being muscle but the intestines were no more than a functionless sinewy rope that barely held together. They didn't remove the organs from the cavity, only moving them here and there with a probe, to get a visual of the havoc that the virus had created. It was as though it hit them in the same way at the same time, realizing that once someone was infected it would be too late to begin any treatment. If there *was* any treatment, it would have to be initiated at the moment of infection. Otherwise, 666 began its consummation too quickly for any treatment to have any effect. The *only* recourse, if there were any, was a vaccine, they thought.

After the post of Dr. Lapides, Dr. Conteh looked at Dr. Kitchen and said, "You're calling this thing 666 couldn't be more precise." Neither of them was followers of any religion, but Isabella wondered to herself if 666 really was the *Seventh Plague* told of in Revelations. "It is going to take an army to stop this, even if it's possible." Dr. Conteh said. "I will notify the CDC Director, who must notify the President. We are beyond caution we have to do a national lockdown immediately."

"Did the corpse have any identification?" Dr. Kitchen said.

"His name was Charles Lapides. And... he was a doc from Wilton, just up north a bit."

"Jesus," Isabella said, "then he contracted 666 from a patient!"

After they cleaned up, Isabella and Aniru, as Dr. Conteh told Isabella to call him, went to the parking area and found the car with a blood-stained seat. They didn't open the doors of the car. Instead, they had hospital security cordon off the area. Then they notified the sheriff. Once he arrived, they told him that the vehicle must be towed to an isolated location and burned. Once it is burned it must be burned again. No one is to touch the car in any way and the driver of the tow truck must gown up before he hooks cable to the car. The security officer at the hospital said he would supervise as Isabella and Aniru had to be on their way to Wilton.

## Chapter 15

"WE HAVE TO FIND where the body is of the patient who exposed Dr. Lapides. That has to be our first task," Isabella said. Aniru agreed. Isabella knew that the person who had exposed Dr. Lapides would *have* to be dead, there could be no mistaking that. So, the question would be what had happened to the body and to those who had handled it. They then began to discuss how the index case had to be figured out above all else. Who was he, where had he come from and where had he been before he came to Wilton? Isabella said that 666 had only been observed in Western Africa, so unless it had migrated to other regions of Africa, the index patient must have immigrated from Liberia to the United States, not long after being infected. Since she left Liberia there had been no known reports of an outbreak.

Before they left, Aniru had called the Wilton sheriff's office saying he and Isabella would be coming to Wilton and for the sheriff to meet them at the edge of town. The dispatcher said that the sheriff had been involved in an emergency and had to go home because he was feeling under the weather. Aniru asked the dispatcher what symptoms the sheriff was reporting. When she related the sheriff's symptoms, Aniru asked the dispatcher to patch a call directly through to the sheriff.

When the sheriff answered the phone, he sounded breathless and weak. Aniru asked if the emergency he had been dealing with involved a man who was very sick. The sheriff confirmed and related what had happened at Dr. Lapides' office and how he had managed to catch the bus before it made it to Washburn. Aniru asked if the sheriff knew what had happened to the dead man's body. Dispatch was to call Flint and Sons Mortuary, pick it up and transport it to the funeral home, he said. The sheriff went on to say he had ordered the bus driver to stay at the Painted Wood Crick pullout. "His name is Joe; he thinks the bus is his ship and he is the captain. Joe won't let anyone leave!"

Isabella got on the phone and asked for the sheriff to describe his symptoms exactly. The sheriff related that along with the intense fever, shaking and weakness, he was beginning to bleed profusely from his rectum, his eyes and spitting up "hunks" of clotted blood. He said he was very weak and asked what he should do. "Do you want me to be direct with you, Sheriff?" Isabella asked him. She heard a moment of silence and then a weak "Yes" on the other end of the phone. Taking a deep breath, Isabella said, "You are dying, sir, and very quickly, likely it is just a matter of hours. There is absolutely *no* possibility you will survive. You have been exposed to something that has *no* cure.

"*If* I was in your position, I would not let this virus kill me, I would take that into my own hands. And... if you choose to do that, please do it in your bathtub with the door closed.

"Sir, I am sorry to sound uncaring, I am just doing my best to protect others, but *please* plug the drain in your tub thoroughly, and sir, I would set the bathroom on fire right before you end your life." The sheriff said he understood.

After they hung up, the sheriff went to his garage, got a can of gas, and once he made his way back to the bathroom, poured it on his bath towels and ignited it. He used the wall to hold himself up and then climbed into the bathtub. He pulled the shower curtain around the tub and pushed the rubber stopper tightly into the drain with his foot. After a momentary hesitation, the sheriff took his service revolver and shot himself in the head.

Isabella called Flint and Sons asking the woman answering the phone if the men who went to collect the deceased man from Dr. Lapides' office were still at the funeral home. The woman said they were just readying to leave. Isabella told her to stop them immediately and to find out if they had stopped anywhere in between Dr. Lapides' office and the funeral home and for them to remain where they were. No one was allowed to leave, it was quarantined. The woman asked Isabella to wait while she checked with the men about their route after they picked up the body. Both men confirmed they brought the dead man right back, needing badly to change their clothes and wash up before going home. Again, Isabella stressed to the woman that under CDC orders no one was to leave the funeral home, and no one was allowed to enter, until they heard from her directly. Then Aniru and Isabella set out for Wilton.

# Chapter 16

ISABELLA AND ANIRU DECIDED to drive directly to the bus and then, depending on what they found, go on to the funeral home. In about thirty minutes or so, they saw the bus at the Painted Wood Crick turnout.

There was no movement outside of the bus and the vacuum door was closed. Isabella and Aniru parked away from the bus and sat and watched for a while. They could see no one moving inside and passengers' heads resting against the windows. When they walked toward the front of the bus, they saw Joe with his head seemingly stuck in between the spokes of the steering wheel, lolled to one side, dried blood pooled around his mouth, eyes, and nose. It was obvious from looking through the glass in the door that his seat and the floor beneath it was soaked with bloody diarrhea. As they went around the bus they pounded on each window where a body sat. Each person looked the same from the shoulders up. Isabella and Aniru imagined each passenger also looked like Joe from the shoulders down. There was no response from any of the people who had been unfortunate to have taken this particular bus. Isabella looked at Aniru and said, "We have to burn it..." There was no question, no arguing, only a mutual understanding from what they had seen and been through that this was the only way.

They decided that Isabella should take the car and drive to Washburn to get several cans of gasoline, that Aniru, being black, would likely be questioned and not safe if he went by himself. The road to Washburn was almost devoid of traffic. Aniru would stay out of sight in case the highway patrol came by. Should he have to, Aniru would present his ID and keep the officer away from the bus.

Isabella drove another fifteen miles or so, bought three five-gallon

41

gas cans, filled them at a local filling station and made her way back to the bus. When she arrived, Aniru told her no one had come by. Aniru ripped the carpet lining from the trunk of the car, soaked it in gasoline and pushed it under the bus. Then Isabella poured gas over the sides of the bus, making sure as much as she could that it seeped down between the bus frame and the window wells. Aniru then pried open the engine compartment and soaked it with one of the cans of gas. Isabella lit the saturated trunk carpet ablaze. They also immolated the boy Joe had thrown off the bus, who now lay dead by the creek. They drove away a safe distance, watching the flames eventually consuming the bus and all the corpses inside.

After an hour, with no vehicles having traversed the road, Aniru and Isabella approached the charred bus. Having donned their masks, gloves and boots, they pulled off the remnants of the door and made their way up and down the aisle dousing each body, already burned beyond recognition with the one can of gas they had saved for this purpose. Then they set them on fire. It was simply too risky not to do this final step. They both had learned this in the jungles and now even though they were far away from Africa, they were in the throes of a different type of war in a different kind of jungle.

After Isabella and Aniru were satisfied that the passengers on the bus posed no risk, should someone come upon them, they made their way to Flint and Sons. They also talked about the hell that they were setting off with what they were doing on their own. Isabella had informed the CDC Director before she left Atlanta, saying that he *must* notify the President about the situation. Assuming what Dr. Conteh surmised was correct about what he was now involved in, this was an international emergency and the military had to be apprised and mobilized. The Director responded that it was far too early to engage in what was likely a hysterical reaction to something that was not even confirmed to be a virus, much less the 666 Virus, it could after all be a toxic exposure of some type, but indeed it was far too early to begin widespread panic or at worse... the CDC, not to mention the President looking foolish. Plus, he said, "You know Dr. Kitchen, many people found the paper you wrote, well, questionable at best, viruses simply do not behave as you described, I, as you are aware, remain skeptical as well. But I guess someone read it and found it compelling... Let me know what you find, once you have an opportunity to investigate..."

Shortly after Isabella and Aniru entered Wilton, they made their way to Dr. Lapides' office, which sat right on the main drag through town. They put on masks and gloves and put booties over their shoes. Isabella, when she had gone to get the cans of gas, also bought as much bleach as she could find.

The door to Dr. Lapides' clinic was not locked, in fact the front door wasn't even latched. It was obvious where the index case had died. There was a large area where the carpet in the waiting room was caked with blood and thick, muck-like tissue. Opening the bottles of bleach, Isabella and Aniru poured the bottles in a three-foot cir-cumference beyond the blood, letting it hopefully kill anything that had splattered out to that perimeter. Then they soaked the primary area caked in blood.

"There isn't much more we can do unless we burn the place down," Isabella said. "Let's see if there are any medical supplies we need before we leave."

As they made their way to the supply room, they found five gallons of ethyl-alcohol, one of the most potent virucidal agents. When Aniru pulled the bottles from the shelf, Isabella said, "At least it is something, but we don't even know if this will kill what we are dealing with. I sure as hell hope the bleach worked."

In Dr. Lapides' office, Aniru found a .38 revolver and a box of cartridges. He showed it to Isabella and put it in his jacket pocket. Both looked at each other, knowing it was more for them as a last resort than for anyone else.

Once they arrived at Flint and Sons, they discovered the front door to the funeral home was ajar. The first thing they noticed was the utter silence, "...deaf as a ghost," Isabella said.

"Jesus, we just burned a bus full of dead bodies, *but* this place is eerie..." Aniru responded.

Laying just beyond the entrance, were the two bodies of the hearse drivers. As they worked their way through the viewing parlor, they saw a body laid out ready for a viewing that would never come. In the office beyond a black curtain, a woman was sprawled onto the floor, her head wedged between a trash can and a file cabinet. Searching the other rooms, they found no one else, alive at least. From beyond a closed door in the unloading garage lay the body of an old lady. An evacuation trocar was inserted in the jugular with the aspirator still running. Aniru reached over and turned off the machine. Isabella went out to the garage and looked at the electrical panels, "What are you looking for..." Aniru asked her.

"I want to make sure there isn't an evacuation fan somewhere that could be discharging this thing to the outside air." The only fan that was listed by a circuit breaker was the one under the autopsy and it wasn't running.

Aniru went into the prep room and checked the temp of the morgue refrigerator and adjusted it down to – 20 C. He also found the body of the man who had first appeared at Dr. Lapides' office. His mostly liquified corpse was laying on a slab in the cooler. He felt for any identification that the man may have had on him. When he reached into the man's front pocket, Aniru pulled out the corpse's passport. Opening it he saw the "Admitted" stamp showing that he had entered the U.S. one year earlier! How could this be? Aniru thought. He closed the passport, dropped it into the body bag and zipped it back up.

Isabella and Aniru placed the dead hearse drivers and the woman from the office in body bags, put them on a mortuary stretcher and wheeled them into the cooler. The bodies should be frozen in a few hours. A fifty-gallon drum of bleach, with a hand pump, was close to the prep room door. Aniru filled three-gallon bottles and doused the area. Once they were satisfied that the bodies or the facility wasn't an immediate danger, they locked everything down and put a sign on the door, saying the funeral parlor was closed and for no one to enter.

As they left, Aniru said to Isabella, "I have something to tell you, but it makes no sense. The index patient was named Khalid Amaechi." That immediately struck Isabella as ironic given that Khalid was a North African name of Arab decent that meant *deathless* and Amaechi meant *he who knows of tomorrow*. "But..." Aniru said, "his passport was in his pocket, it said he came to the U.S. about a year ago."

"That can't be!" Isabella retorted. "Dear God, if that's true then this thing can lay dormant for who knows how long and then spring to life with vengeance!"

Isabella called into to the head of the CDC. She notified him of the situation and what they had done to "hopefully" encapsulate the virus for the moment. But clearly, they had not resolved anything about what the hell was going on. "Have you notified the President of the situation?" Isabella asked.

"That's not your concern! The proper notifications will be made when and if I make the determination to do so..."

At that point Isabella began clicking the hook switch saying they had a bad connection and hung up the phone. When she got back in the car, Isabella looked at Aniru and said, "bastard... They are going to do nothing, and this is exploding in our face. I hate politicians..."

It had become cliche to paint the CDC as an agency whose focus was mainly on pleasing who was in the seat of power at the time than one whose primary concern was monitoring the outbreak of potential epidemics and keeping the country safe from biological annihilation. But, after the HIV debacle, there wasn't much more that could be said in terms of the agencies attempt to resurrect itself. And now... with the emergence of the 666 Virus, Isabella and Aniru were sitting on what could be the greatest loss of life the world had ever known. *If* anyone survived.

It wasn't long after Isabella had called the CDC director a bastard when her pager when off, indicating it was an emergency call. The number was the direct line to the CDC director.

"Jesus, do you think he heard me?" Isabella said to Aniru.

"Not unless he is telepathic..." Aniru responded.

He found a pay phone and pulled the car to the curb. When Isabella called, the CDC director said she was to go immediately to Fargo. Apparently one of the hospital ERs were reporting a half-dozen patients who presented in the past 24 hours with 666 symptoms. Now all were deceased. They were about three hours from Fargo. Isabella told the director to contact the Chief of Staff at the hospital and lock it down. No one leaves the hospital and all infectious disease emergency procedures were to be immediately implemented.

As they were leaving Wilton, Aniru stopped the car and turned around in the middle of the road. "There is something that is bothering me," he said. "I want to go back and look more closely at the index patient. I want you to help me."

"Why?" Isabella asked inquisitively.

"I recognize his name, I don't remember how or why, but I know I do... I think there is something wrong here, beside what we have found... I don't fully understand..."

When they arrived back at the funeral home, they gowned up and went straight to the cooler and removed Khalid's body. "What are we looking for, there is not much here..." Isabella said. Aniru looked down at Khalid's body and responded, "I have no idea." He then retrieved his passport and wallet, finding nothing else in his pockets. When he opened the wallet, he read the name on his identification card and immediately recalled why Khalid's name was familiar. "Now I recognize his name..." Aniru said to Isabella. "Why... Look at his ID card." Then Aniru raised the wallet and said, "Jesus!" The identification card read: Khalid Amaechi, Ph.D. Research Scientist, Dugway Proving Ground, U.S. Army Garrisons, Dugway, UT.

At that point, Isabella said, "Something is wrong, what the hell is *he* doing in Wilton, ND? And why is he dead from whatever this is? This makes no sense," Isabella told Aniru. "We have to search every part of his body... He was at a top-secret facility, having something on his body would be the only way he could have gotten something past security..."

Aniru nodded in agreement. Aniru turned Dr. Amaechi over, giving Isabella access to his rectum. She inserted a finger into his anus and immediately felt something hard with a flattened surface. Isabella raised the rectal tissue, allowing her finger to get beyond whatever she was feeling and slipped it out of his anal sphincter. There in her hand was a small stainless cylinder. Aniru, astonished, looked at Isabella and said, "What... in the hell *is* that?"

"I don't know but I think we need to get out of here now."

They quickly zipped the body bag back up, took his ID, passport, and the cylinder, and placed them in a biohazard bag. Isabella went and rifled through the lap drawer of where the dispatcher's coat was hanging. There she found a set of car keys. "Let's leave our car and take whatever car this one fits, probably parked outback." Aniru nodded in agreement. Before they left, Aniru said "Let me pull my car around the corner." Isabella smiled and said, "That's in a neighborhood in rural North Dakota. They'd probably throw you to the ground and hold you for their local sheriff who'd just likely shot himself..."

"Let me, and I will walk right back..." Aniru wryly smiled and nodded his head. When Isabella got back into the dispatcher's car, Aniru said, "You were none too subtle..." To which Isabella said, "I am more subtle than your blackness, in the heart of rural white

America with a Nigerian accent..." Then each smiled at the other as Aniru began the drive out of town.

After they were a few minutes down the road, a cluster of trees came into view with an access road that Aniru and Isabella figured were used for lovers looking for some privacy in the barren landscape. Aniru pulled behind the cluster, turned off the car, and for just a moment, he and Isabella lay their heads against the back of the seats and closed their eyes. In a short while they got out of the car. Isabella retrieved a jug of sodium hypochlorite she had taken from the mortuary from the trunk of the car. She and Aniru put on gloves, donned a mask and a face shield. Aniru held the biohazard bag open while Isabella poured the sodium hypochlorite over the stainless cannister. Isabella then gently rotated the bag ensuring that the liquid would encompass every aspect of the container. Then they sat it aside for thirty minutes.

After they were assured that no hemorrhagic virus could survive in the liquid environment in the biohazard bag, they dug a foot deep hole, poured the sodium hypochlorite into the dried dirt, and dropped the bag inside the hole. Isabella filled the hole back in. There sitting on the ground was the capsule that had been hidden in Dr. Amaechi's rectum. For a brief moment, they sat looking at the container, then at each other. Keeping their gloves, mask, and face shields on, Aniru picked up the cylinder and began unscrewing the top. Not sure what to expect, he made sure the opening of the container was pointed away from both him and Isabella. When the top came off, there was no liquid, no pellets, nothing that would indicate that there was any biological material inside. Rather, there was a tightly rolled piece of paper. Small script was written on the page. After being in Western Africa, Isabella had a familiarity with many of the main languages but this was one that she didn't recognize.

"Do you know it?" Isabella asked Aniru.

"Yes, it is Bakpinka, it is one of the dying languages of the Upper Cross Rivers... It is becoming increasingly rare to see it used anywhere, even in the place of its birth. He must have written this deliberately in Bakpinka so it couldn't easily be translated and understood." As they sat side-by-side, Aniru began to translate the script.

*To whom it may concern, Clearly, if you are reading this, I am* dead and I have died because of the virus that has consumed me.

Let me explain. I am Khalid Amaechi, Ph.D., I am a research scientist who specialized in the genetic modification of viruses. I have been working on the combining of Zaire Ebola and Marburg Virus and into a distinct virus entity. I then additionally altered the measles virus to its most virulent form which resulted in a stable form of measles induced subacute sclerosing panencephalitis. From there I combined the three virus entities into a superinfectant viral agent. This was done for the purpose of using this agent as a biological weapon should such a devastating global warfare need arise. The problem that presented itself was of course that such a viral entity would be unstoppable once unleashed. Therefore, the development of a vaccine and what would be required for inoculation of those not impacted on the battlefield was not practical. What was required was a mechanism of activating and deactivating the newly developed virus, so that even once the virus had successfully infected a host, it could in essence be deactivated, should it not have progressed to the point of destroying the individual's immune system, making recovery impossible. However, its viability as an infectious agent would be nullified.

We discovered the long-discredited work of an individual named Royal R. Rife. He made many claims that were scientifically non-sensical, but in examining some of his ideas using UHF and EHF waves to influence microbial and viral behaviour we were able to adapt his work to where we used UHF to activate the newly developed virus and EHF to deactivate the virus. This way we could use this form of battlefield incapacitation without risking a massive civilian catastrophe. This work was done at Dugway Proving Ground, Utah. There was a human trials exposure of selected villages in western Africa a few years ago. The viral entity, which I have learned was euphemistically called the 666 Virus in a paper describing its clinical effects, which we had to discredit to maintain security, was in fact correct in terms of its case fatality rate being 100% with there being no means of treatment, realistically other than rapid euthanasia of the victims. The descriptions of the viral infection, incubation and ultimately its mortality was however completely accurate. Once a host is infected, the virus will lay dormant until such a time where it is activated by exposure to an oscillating electrical field matching the frequency of the new viral entity. Each exposure profile sets a new UHF frequency oscillation. The exposure protocol consists of the virus being aerosolized and distributed within specific geographic parameters. In war, this of course would be the coordinates of a respective battlefield. The UHF and EHF equations set for the generator were on a need to know only basis and top secret. There was a limited team of scientists on this project. The area in western Africa chosen for exposure were several tribes where there was at least a three-mile circumference between village one, village two and so on. Understand the UHF frequency was not discernable by auditory means. Only mammals are affected by the viral entity. Any other species are not affected. Factually, the tribes that were chosen were considered by Dugway to be dying out, primarily because of inbreeding. We made the decision that their loss was a sacrifice that was justified by the number of lives that would be saved if a war was becoming ob-viously unwinnable. The viral entity could also have been used on cities and critical nuclear enclaves that were impenetrable by other means. The results of the experiment were considered a success. Then a special detail division of the army was brought in to destroy any evidence that could have possibly been associated with the project. After the villages were incinerated the EHF was broadcast over a hundred-mile radius effectively counterposing the UHF. It was then that we vacated the area and returned with our data to Dugway. Once we fully analyzed our intelligence it was decided we had an effective and deployable weapon should a national security situation arise. When the article, that we even-tually discredited was published, we adopted 666 as its name, believing it was as accurate and fitting as any other. I left Dugway shortly after that, retiring if you will, to Fargo, it being about as nothing of a place as I could imagine to disappear. All was fine until a few days ago, when I began to show signs of being infect-ed with 666. Of course, I contacted the commander of Dugway who told me that was impossible. I assured him that being one of 666s primary developers, I fully knew what was happening to me and he needed to find an explanation as I would not be alive long enough to do so. Although our development team took every precaution against becoming infected, obviously we failed. But, *outside of the lab there would be no way of the virus becoming activated. So, it wouldn't be a matter of the virus lying dormant, it simply, for all practical purposes, wouldn't exist. The likely most important question scientifically is not how I and likely others became infected, but how was the virus activated? My thinking is clearly becoming impacted but I have decided that the best way for me to bring attention to this, and in essence kill as few as people as possible, is to board a bus to a more remote town. Like before, that a few must be sacrificed in order to bring about a solution for the many, so that the entire planet does not perish. It must also be said that we (collectively the Dugway Research Group) did so under the specific order of the President of the United States and under the ultimate direction of a biological weapons expert, Dr. Theodore Prokiv. Be that as it may, I hope I am not too late. Khalid Amaechi, Ph.D.*

Aniru and Isabella sat for a few moments, looking at each other, without speaking.

Isabella spoke first, "Jesus Christ, what are we up against, how did Dr. Amaechi become infected in the first place, who and why did 666 become activated and... we have to assume, although he didn't say as much, that once the virus reaches a certain level in the activated patient, 666 becomes infectious regardless of any EHF intervention to stop it."

Aniru then followed, "So when the EHF is introduced, regardless of where the patient is in the infectious cycle, the virus will cease becoming infectious, but also depending upon where the infected patient is in the infected process, that will determine whether they will live or die and what kind of lasting effects, if they live, they will have. My God, why in the hell would *anyone* in their right mind, create something like this? It's barbaric..." Aniru looked puzzled for a moment, "Then the people on the bus, those in the funeral home and Dr. Lapides were all infected because 666 had not been disabled by a corresponding EHF. But, if say the people on the bus became infected shortly after Dr. Amaechi boarded the bus, but then just as quickly the virus was turned off by generating an encoded electro-magnetic frequency, then those people would not be infectious until they were exposed to the UHF. But... they would still be carrying an inert copy of the virus somewhere in their DNA. And," Aniru said, "the way technology is advancing, who knows when one of them would encounter a UHF that would in fact activate the fucking virus!"

Filled with angst, Isabella immediately thought of Chidinma and how she had been the only one in the village that had not died. Even though she had conducted the usual tests on Chidinma, she knew now there was no way to know if in fact she harbored the virus or not. The only way she would know is if she developed symptoms.

# Chapter 17

Isabella and Aniru decided to get a room for the night to clean up and to plan their next move. She had been out of contact with the CDC now and she was sure they were trying to contact her. She would check in with her secretary in the morning. They pulled off Rt 36 into a parking lot that seemingly had a pasture of weeds growing between the cracks in the concrete. There was only one other car. When they rang the bell, a young girl came from the office adjacent to the check in area. When she saw Aniru and then Isabella, she said in a strained smoky voice, "What can I do for you?"

"We would like a room for the night."

"Are you two married?" the smoky-mouth girl asked.

Aniru looked at Isabella and said, "Yes, we are on our honeymoon." They both signed in with 'M.D.' after their names. Isabella looked at the girl and said, "I don't suppose you have anyone to carry our luggage?" And, with that, the key landed precisely in one of the many cigarette divots that had burned a memory of guests gone by into the linoleum countertop.

Isabella put her arm through Aniru's and said, "Come, darling, let's get to our room."

The girl watched them with obvious disdain. When they reached the door of the room, Isabella slipped the key into the lock, as Aniru picked her up, pushed the door open with his foot and carried her over the threshold. As he let Isabella down, she said, "What *bullshit* to have to put up with!"

Aniru said, "It will never go away." Isabella looked at Aniru and said, "I think it would be a shame if we didn't consummate our marriage."

They slowly undressed, savoring each moment, taking each other to erotic heights throughout the night, and found what they had been long searching for in another. In the morning, as they were preparing to leave, Isabella put her arms around Aniru and said, "Just a few hours ago we were contemplating the end of the world and right now I see my world so all-embracing that I simply can't believe it."

"I know it will sound like a cliche, but..." Still embraced and never moving their eyes from the other, Aniru said,

> "*From my very roots*
> *my allegiance to you I vow.*
> *I wallow in your fruits*
> *and to your very presence I bow.*
> *In awe of you I stand*
> *before a love...*
> *never again to be found.*"

Aniru took the key back to the office, dropped it on the counter, as Isabella pulled the car up front. A turn here and a turn there and they were back on 36.

# Chapter 18

"SO WHERE ARE THIS Dr. Conteh and Dr. Kitchen now?"

"Sir, we haven't actually heard from them for three days, since Dr. Kitchen was contacted by Dr. Conteh, but we believe they are still in North Dakota, and we have alerted the local and state police to stop them and have them brought back here on a mission essential basis."

"You have a black man with a white woman in North Dakota somewhere, that can't be too goddamn hard to find them... Jesus, I don't care what the hell you have to do, but *find* them."

"Yes..." was the only answer the Director of the CDC could possibly give to the president.

It wasn't long after they were driving east on 36 when Isabella saw a state highway patrol car sitting in the medium. As they passed, the patrol car immediately pulled out with its lights flashing and coming up behind them, with the officer waving for them to pull over. When they pulled to the berm of the highway, the patrol officer jumped from his car and ran towards Isabella and Aniru's car. Isabella retrieved her CDC identification, rolled down the window and put both arms out. The highway patrol officer was waving his hands, back and forth seemingly saying that wasn't necessary. When he reached their car, the officer said, "...are you folks Dr. Isabella Kitchen and Dr. Aniru Conteh?"

Isabella answered that yes, they were.

"You are needed back in Washington D.C. for an emergency meeting. This came through our office with the highest priority. I ordered a highway patrol chopper. They should be here in about twenty minutes or so and they will take you folks to the Minot Base, and they will get you on over to D.C. Do you know what this is all about?" the officer asked.

Dr. Conteh looked out and said, "Thank you for finding us and making the arrangements but... we really can't talk about it.

"Is there some kind of infection we should know about or some danger to our family?"

"As you know, I am Dr. Conteh, and this is Dr. Kitchen, and we would tell you if we believed there was an immediate risk for anyone. Thank you, again, for your prompt action."

It was less time than the highway patrol thought it would be that the chopper landed and Isabella and Aniru were aboard and airborne headed up to Minot Army Base. A C-130 outbound was ordered rerouted to Fort McNair Army Base. It took about five hours from takeoff to landing. Isabella and Aniru had been sitting on nylon webbed sling seats. At one point Isabella had leaned over to Aniru and said, "My ass hurts." In the cargo hold area, the turbulence was felt with a vengeance. Neither thought much of flying.

The President's Chief of Staff met them at McNair. Each was greeted with the perfunctory smile and "Hello Dr. Conteh and Dr. Kitchen, it is a pleasure to meet you. The President is looking forward to your arrival." As they walked up the ramp to board Marine One, the Chief of Staff said, "We will be going up to Camp David, not the West Wing." They were both brought a change of clothes, something the Chief of Staff considered more appropriate.

The flight took a little more than thirty minutes. They were met by two secret service agents and two marine escorts. Another marine guard took Isabella's hand as she stepped into the golf cart that would take them to their meeting with the president.

In but a few minutes they arrived at what looked like an old, pleasantly preserved farmhouse. When they entered through the front door, they immediately passed through a magnetometer and then wanded by a secret service agent. Finding the .38, the secret service agent looked suspiciously at Aniru. "It's so we can shoot *ourselves*, if necessary, not the president..." Aniru said to him.

"You can have it back when you leave," he was told.

"The President will be with you momentarily," the Chief of Staff announced. A short while later, a marine appeared from another hallway and indicated by the wave of his hand that they were to follow. They entered an elevator around the corner from where they were sitting. There were only two buttons on the panel, one up and one down. The Chief of Staff pushed the down button. There was no indication of how far down they had been taken. The only indication they had arrived was when the elevator doors opened onto a long, well-lit hallway. A marine stood outside of one of the doors. A few steps down, the marine turned and saluted the Chief of Staff and opened the first door to the Camp David situation room. The first room resembled an airlock, they could hear the door they had just come through seal behind them. Then the Chief of Staff looked up at the imbedded camera in one corner of the room, nodded his head and the inner door now opened. The President, the head of the CDC and another man, were seated at a long table, surrounded by empty chairs. In front of three of the chairs were leather portfolios with the presidential seal on the cover.

Isabella and Aniru were directed to sit down in front of the designated portfolios. As of yet, no words had been spoken. After a few moments of silence, the President stood up and spoke. "Drs. Kitchen and Conteh, welcome and thank you for coming.

"Dr. Conteh, you obviously have no clearance status, but given the circumstances of what you have uncovered and of course and most importantly your expertise, we have decided to bring you in. Please understand, Dr. Conteh, that what we are about to discuss here never leaves this situation room. And Dr. Kitchen, you have a top-secret clearance from your work at the CDC. The portfolios in front of you outline what we are about to discuss.

"Seated beside me, as you are aware, Dr. Kitchen, is Dr. Foege, Director of the CDC, and to introduce you, this is Dr. Theodore Prokiv. Dr. Prokiv was brought in because he began his work on chemical and biological weapons systems at Dugway laboratory, outside of Salt Lake, was the Chief of Chemical and Biological Weapons Development, and simultaneously focused his work on whatever was developed, there had to be an equally effective means of destroying it. That of course is why he is here. I have decided, given the nature of what appears to be manifesting, to keep these events strictly on a need-to-know basis. I have notified the head of the CIA and the Joint Chiefs, strictly as a precaution, with limited information, should it become necessary to have them more involved. Likely that determination will be made during this meeting. I would like to turn the meeting over to Dr. Prokiv."

"Dr. Kitchen, Dr. Conteh, your works speak for itself. Dr. Kitchen, your clinical conclusions were indeed correct in your post-Liberian work, and I apologize that the Defense Department found it necessary to, for the most part, discredit your conclusions. It was in the interest of national security. And Dr. Conteh, as the President said, you obviously became involved in this in an ancillary manner, but given your expertise in hemorrhagic fevers, and what you have now seen, and as I understand, discovered via the death of Dr. Khalid Amaechi, we believe it is as imperative that you be here as much as Dr. Kitchen."

Dr. Prokiv continued, "I first became affiliated with DPG as a young Army officer, right after I obtained my Ph.D. in biophysical chemistry. I was brought in actually to focus on how to structurally develop chemical and biological weapons for both offensive and defensive purposes. It was my goal to deduce how it would be possible to use a chemical means of activating a biological response. Similar means have been used before, but I wanted something that would be seamless, if you will, and that would at the same time be something we could both activate, and when the need arose, deactivate.

"I brought in a group of scientists who were very narrowly focused in their specializations. But it wasn't long before we realized that everything we tried either was successful on one side but failed on the other, or vice versa. Then Dr. Amaechi happened upon an article by Dr. Royal Rife about activating viruses with ultra-high frequencies and deactivating them with extremely high frequencies. Of course, this sounded like a lunatic talking. Dr. Amaechi began to work on this on his own and then approached me with startling results. He had combined two hemorrhagic fevers with measles, recoded their chemical structure and then bioengineered them to respond to either a unique UHF or EHF signal. It was still very rough, theoretically and in application, but the foundation was there. From that moment, we retooled our entire program and focused on refining the process. It was an absolute stroke of genius to combine the hemorrhagic fevers with the measles virus to increase susceptibility. For in that *alone* he made a devastating biochemical weapon. But then to have them activate or deactivate a combination of viruses based upon a unique signal frequency was both diabolical, genius, and in many respects, undefeatable. So, this process was clinically refined, and the first human tests were done on several villages in outer Liberia. I am going to be very blunt about this, but these villages were dying, the populations had decreased because of constant inbreeding, and it was just a matter of time until they disappeared altogether."

Even though most of what Dr. Prokiv was relating Isabella and Aniru already knew from reading the note retrieved from Dr. Amaechi, it was still *chilling* to hear it being presented by one of the world's leading experts on chemical and biological weapons, in the bowels of Camp David and locked in a SCIF, in a frigidly calculating delivery. "Jesus," Isabella thought. Aniru found himself clinching his fists under the table at the barbaric racism and eco-narcissism declaring whole populations simply lab rats to be sacrificed on *kill day*.

As Isabella and Aniru refocused, they heard Dr. Prokiv saying... "After what was deemed a successful test, the tri-part virus was shelved, until, obviously, and why we are all here, with the death of Dr. Lapides. Then the loss of the other lives. It appears as though currently there are more cases that have emerged. We have no idea why that is. But of course, the other critical question is how did Dr. Amaechi get infected in the first place and then how did he become activated? And once he knew he was actively infected, why did he do what he did, namely go to somewhere called Wilton, North Dakota? I have countless questions and no answers. We have DPG on lockdown and radio silence, there is no comm in and no comm out. All communication devices have been confiscated. Any communication in or out must be by secure channels and go directly through the Command Sargent Major."

Aniru then asked, "So Dr. Prokiv, why are we here and what in the hell are you proposing? Most especially after stating emphatically that the United States is guilty of genocide... *Christ, who are you fucking people!*"

Ignoring Aniru, Dr. Prokiv said, "Factually, we do not have any idea what happened and how Dr. Amaechi became infected. If you have any theories, we would welcome hearing those. As far as we have been able to determine, there have been no breaches at the DPG. We do not believe he infected himself, so if others at DPG have been infected, then we have a monumental national security concern. Because someone clearly has the coding frequencies to activate and deactivate the virus. The two of you know more about the clinical manifestations of the virus than anyone, even the scientists who have been working intently on it, as they have not seen it fully activated

58

in a biological specimen."

For a moment, Isabella and Aniru sat and stared at each other. "Christ Almighty," Isabella thought, "This can't be real." And in that same moment where she had hoped thought would win out, she imagined herself entering the gates of a long-abandoned cemetery where the graves of the dead had been desecrated and, *who* those the bones once were had vanished as though they had never been there in the first place. Then softly shaking her head she returned to the reality of this unreality.

Aniru spoke up and said, "So you know, and I believe I am speaking for the both of us, we only have one concern, and that is stopping the spread of the virus before it continues to kill everything in its path. Dr. Kitchen works for the federal government and I do not. And, after listening to you, Dr. Prokiv, I can't imagine I ever would. You chose to murder countless people on the African continent simply because you considered them *expendable*. You are nothing more than a representable bastard."

Isabella then followed, "As soon as this exercise in debauchery is over, one way or another, I am resigning my commission with the CDC. The way I see it, you people can't do anything without Dr. Conteh and myself. The first thing I am doing is to leave here and get my daughter in Atlanta, who will remain with Dr. Conteh and myself as we try and figure out what we are going to do and how we are going to do it. Secondly, if we say we want something, information or otherwise, the first bit of bullshit, the first lie or the first '...we can't give you that information because it is classified,' then regardless of the consequences, we *are* done. I don't care if you are the President, I don't care if you are the head of the CDC and I could care less who you are, Dr. Prokiv, these are our terms."

The President leaned forward and said, "You can have any access to anything you want. If you encounter *any* interference from anyone for any reason, you contact me directly. You will have *complete* access to any of us at any time. I understand your positions and respect them. I also want to inform you that an aftermath crew was dispatched to North Dakota and the tragic bus accident, the events at the funeral home, the hospital where you were consulting Dr. Conteh, Dr. Lapides' death and the death of the sheriff have all been resolved. Nothing more needs to be discussed, suffice to say, we will leave it at that."

And on that the meeting was adjourned.

# Chapter 19

♪ *Five foot two, A little chunky with eyes of blue, there goes Little Bobby in his unmatched shoes.... won't anybody be his pal...?* ♪

WHENEVER BOBBY WALKED PAST the people in the assembly plant, he invariably heard them humming. He wasn't sure of the words of the tune, but he knew it was disparaging, and... poor Bobby hung his chin to his chest and carried himself on to his office. Bobby was in fact only five foot two and if the truth be known he probably slurred the "two" when he was asked for his height, likely being more like five-foot. He also, no matter what, never wore shoes that matched. For some reason or other, whenever Bobby got dressed in the morning, he always ended up with shoes that didn't match. It'd been that way since he was a boy, from the time he first learned to tie his shoes and it didn't get any better as he got to be a big boy. And now... "Well..." he would say, looking down, when someone mentioned it.

His mother and father had always known he was going to be short, with his little arms, legs and torso never growing very much.

But what he lacked in height he made up in kindness and developed into what the people at his church said was a good and decent boy. "Why that Bobby, he'd give you the shirt off his back, need be." He was never without a kind word for someone, even the *hummers*, who at times there were so many of them that they sounded like a four-part chorus, when he walked by.

Since Bobby had few friends as a child, his mother and father tried to surround his world with toys. Very special toys. Right after Thanksgiving, Marsh's grocery store began to set up their Christmas toy displays. There atop the produce case was *Robot Commander*, fending off an invading army, who didn't stand a chance against his whirling arms, unleashing bombs against the enemy, saving the world again and again. Then the nemesis' planes coming in for a counterattack only to be undone by Robot Commander's secret weapon, the top of his head lifted to reveal a missile, that blew them out of the sky. "Ohhhhhh," Bobby imagined as he stood below the nicely arranged cucumbers and envisioned the battle being played out. Sitting right next to the Robot Commander display was the *Barracuda Submarine*... "Oh my gosh..." Bobby thought, "which do I choose, which do I want more than *anything* in the whole wide world." Bobby's mommy would rest her hand on his shoulder, telling him he would have to choose so they could tell the store manager, who called Santa's elves to let them know what good little boys and girls wanted for Christmas.

That particular year though, Bobby told his mommy that he wanted the Robot Commander and... a *Signal Ray Gun with Three Barrels*. Could Santa bring both "for me?" he said.

And on that very Christmas morning, Santa didn't let Bobby down, for there under the tree was Robot Commander and the greatest ray gun ever made. It shot red, blue, and green rays. If one color didn't destroy the enemy then another would for sure.

Bobby loved his toys that year more than any other year, "ever!" he would proclaim. It was also that year and those very toys that made Bobby want to be a toy designer. To bring that kind of happiness that he had known as a child to other boys. For little boys to be able to give life to their imagination. As he grew into manhood, he went to college, worked hard to get his degree in electrical engineering and got himself a job as the chief toy designer at the biggest toy maker of all time. He always thought he would design the greatest toys that had ever been made. Cars that would go this way and that, directed by the voice of a boy he had made so happy. Robots, robots and more robots, who did everything.

But in his designing of the greatest of all toys, Bobby would go home at night, sit at his design table, and wear out pencil after pencil, trying to figure out the design of the *greatest* ray gun anyone had ever conceived. He didn't want it to hurt anyone. But he did want somehow for the beam of the gun to "tingle" when it landed on its intended adversary. But, "gosh..." he would think to himself, how could he invent such a toy?

Then one night he had gone to his nondescript row house on a nondescript street, in Philadelphia, sat down at his design table, turned on the light that clipped to the edge of his well-etched drafting board and then... it came to him. He had been trying to design a toy. Why not design a real ray gun and then ratchet it down into a toy! He *was* after all an electrical engineer.

And set to work he did, until he had developed a prototype of what he knew would become the toy that would not only bear his name, but win him the most prestigious award of all, *The International Toy Design Award*. Bobby's name would be enshrined with all the great toy designers throughout history. But... as he leaned on his elbow in self-obsessed admiration for the resolution to his problem, Bobby then came nose-to-nose with the monumental difficulty of his solution.

The next day, Bobby asked for permission to set up a small laboratory in the manufacturing plant to work on a toy design that he assured the owner of the company would bring renowned recognition to the toy company. It would be expensive, Bobby said, but... each and every day, Bobby would trod through the plant, past the assembly workers who were busy fitting roving eyeballs into dollies and fenders and roofs onto exploding cars, while he carried his crumbled up papers, slide-rule and his T-square.

It was a wintery afternoon, with a light wind blowing wispy snow here and there when he finally soldered the last capacitor onto the circuit board. He then fit everything into the prototype that resembled the other worldly explorers silver ray guns that the movies of old that had no sound used to defend themselves from nameless creatures inhabiting other planets. Bobby decided that all the ray gun had to do was to generate a very high frequency sound, one so high that it was unable to be heard by the human ear, but would produce radio waves much greater than 1 GHz, which would cause a kind of radiation dermatitis, which of course sounded worse than it really was. When boys, who were just being boys, shot their new ray guns at each other, small welts would raise up on the skin and... for a few minutes would itch and then go away. Then it wasn't a matter of one boy arguing with the other about being shot, and then saying " Unh unh." If he was itching, then he'd been shot, and the other boy would have won the battle! The other thing that Bobby decided to do was to add a secret code to his ray gun, which he now called The Garin

Death Ray Pistol, or the GDRP. Which he would have stenciled on the side when it was manufactured. When he was growing up, *The Garin Death Ray* was his favorite book, about a man who creates a remarkable invention which gives him absolute power over others throughout the world. The secret code, which was pulling the trigger three times in a row, waiting ten seconds and then pulling it two more times, caused the GDRP to play the tune, "*Five foot two, A little chunky with eyes of blue, there goes Little Bobby in his unmatched shoes.... won't anybody be his pal.*" Now each and every time he walked past the assembly workers, and they began humming, he would be able to smile to himself, knowing it was *he* who had the last laugh.

Bobby would of course have to prove the worthiness of his design. He set off one afternoon, driving cross country to both go where he had not been and to shoot people with the GDRP. He knew he couldn't just pull out a ray gun and begin shooting, regardless if it was a toy. Someone would mistake it for a real gun, call the police and he could end up being shot. So, before he left, he mounted the ray gun in his briefcase. All he had to do was to point the case at his target and push a small button that he had rigged right next to the soft leather handle. But he made sure that he had turned off the sound effects.

A few days before Dr. Khalid Amaechi started getting sick, Bobby boarded a bus in Philadelphia, destined for Fargo, North Dakota. He had intended to go south, but the buses were full. The Fargo bus only had a few passengers.

## Chapter 20

MARINE ONE TOOK ISABELLA and Aniru to National Airport, where they caught a flight to Atlanta. With a tail wind they were descending into the Atlanta airport in about two hours. Chidinma had come to the airport to meet Isabella and Aniru. In but a short time, Chidinma was wondering who the man was who looked like her, and had accompanied her mother to Atlanta. After a few moments, Isabella introduced Aniru and told Chidinma they were going to be traveling together. An emergency had come about, and she wanted Chidinma with them. In another few hours the three of them would be back in Fargo.

While Isabella, Aniru and Chidinma were in the air, each member of the Dugway group were being interrogated again. There appeared nothing to be found. Each member of the development group gave no indication of being disgruntled or vengeful in their attitudes toward the United States government.

# Chapter 21

WHEN BOBBY ARRIVED IN Fargo, he missed the bottom step of the bus and fell into the driver, adorned in his official gray pants and white shirt. He shoved Bobby aside, saying something about he needed to learn how to walk. Bobby regained his balance, brushed himself off, sat his briefcase on one of the open doors of the bus's luggage hold, pointed the concealed prototype of the GDRP at the driver and pushed the button. Even though Bobby had turned off the sound he still made the oscillating wave sound to himself. In but a few seconds the bus driver began itching. Bobby thought he looked like a monkey in a cage, scratching just about anywhere his hands could reach. He even pulled his tie aside to be able to scratch his chest.

Then just as quickly, Bobby let go of the button. In but another few seconds, the disrespectful, or so Bobby thought, bus driver stopped itching. The other passengers who were still milling around the bus had congregated, watching him, thinking that he might have been having some sort of epileptic fit. One passenger was heard saying, "If he starts foaming at the mouth everybody run, because he's probably been bitten by a rabid bat or something." There were no signs of bats or a *something* anywhere.

Bobby took his briefcase in hand and walked away to get a motel, needing to figure out what to do next. As he walked from the bus station, Bobby began to reflect on what had just happened. He stopped at a cross walk, took a deep breath, and realized he was standing taller, his shoulders weren't slumped over and even though he hadn't said a word, the voice that he used to talk with himself sounded deeper. It was right as the green Walk-Sign changed from *Don't Walk* to *Walk* that Bobby decided from that point on he would be called Robert.

Even though he had not expected it, the feeling he had garnered from watching the bus driver, scratching, and dancing around like a damn fool, made him feel a mightiness that he had never felt before. It wasn't even a sense of feeling fearsome, there was really no sense about it. When Robert pushed the hidden button on his brief case and the driver immediately *snapped-to* in response to being struck by the frequency generated by the GDRP, he imagined himself to be the commander of a battalion of soldiers, who when he entered the room, *snapped-to* attention and remained so, for however long, depending upon his very whim. The itching, "God, the itching..." Robert said to himself, delighted.

# Chapter 22

IT WAS LATE IN the afternoon when Dr. Khalid Amaechi went to an early dinner at an African restaurant he frequented. There he was greeted by the owner, who waved him to his regular window seat. He pushed the menu aside, indicating that he would like his usual order of jabaati with beans with malawah bread and then settled into his seat.

Dr. Amaechi pulled an article from his shoulder bag and began reading about the little-known toxicity of morel mushrooms. People would go out in droves, acting like savage dogs, even pulling guns on each other, in order to scrounge for morels. "Fools," he thought. "Then they would take their prize homes, prepare them in whatever way they thought 'the best...' and then some of them, in a few hours, would begin throwing up, finally succumbing to violent seizures and heart failure, from hydrazine poisoning. "Stupidity should be classified as an epidemic..." he thought. As he sat eating, a short man, carrying a well-scarred briefcase, came in. He was wearing thick horn-rimmed glasses, and his hair was disheveled.

Dr. Amaechi took notice that the man seemed to be unnaturally erect, holding himself almost at attention. When the owner seated him, the man nodded and then waved the owner away, in such an odd way that he looked comedic. After looking at the menu, the slight of height man motioned for the owner to come back to his table. Robert, after the long bus ride, wanted pancakes. The owner explained that his was an African eatery and he did not serve pancakes. Robert became increasingly agitated. He couldn't explain it, it was just that he liked to live a very simple life, and he never wanted anything unless he could have it now. And now he wanted pancakes, with lots of butter, sausage and a "big order of fried potatoes.

"That is not unreasonable..." Robert said to the restauranter, except of course the restaurant didn't have what he wanted. The owner tried to explain, that there was a quaint breakfast place just down the street. Robert, now furious, shoved his chair back hard, raised his briefcase and pointed it toward the owner and Dr. Amaechi, who was not sitting far away. Then he pushed the button. Both Dr. Amaechi and the owner of the restaurant began manically itching. This time though, Robert now enraged, held down on the button and fanned the briefcase left and right. In but a few seconds the cook came out from behind the swinging door to the kitchen, scratching himself, trying to reach places that his arms weren't meant to reach. Dr. Amaechi had no idea what was happening to him, only that he like the restaurant owner, and now the cook, were itching and scratching themselves. The only one who wasn't affected was the little man who had the angry outburst.

As Robert held down the button and watched the spectacle he was creating, he began laughing. *Never* had he laughed so hard. Then, he let up on the button and walked out the door. The cook collapsed on the floor, feeling like he had been burned, then began screaming, "*Popobawa, Popobawa...*" over and over again. He had recently come from Tanzania, where he had encountered the *Popobawa* and believed *it* had followed him to the United States. As his itching subsided, the cook began to cry hysterically, being sure he was the target of a malevolent shapeshifter. The restaurant owner lay quiet on the floor, breathing heavily from scratching himself. Blood trickled down his arms from his abrasions.

Dr. Amaechi, although beginning to recover from the misery of the itching, was curious. "What... had just happened?" He was a scientist; he did not believe in evil spirits. It had all begun when the little angry man began to wave his briefcase around. When the man began laughing, Dr. Amaechi thought him insane. It was odd, but for a moment Dr. Amaechi became concerned that the odd behaving man had used high frequency radio waves to cause the itching mayhem. Then he became concerned that if that were the case that to produce such a violent physiological reaction he must have somehow generated extremely high-level UHF and EHF to disrupt the natural electromagnetic waves of mitochondrial proteins. "Jesus, this is what we were working on at Dugway." Then Dr. Amaechi set aside such a ludicrous thought. He got up and tended to the owner of the restaurant and the still distraught cook, who had grabbed a fork from one of the tables, to scratch his back. Dr. Amaechi, believing he had done what he could, then walked out the door.

≈

# Chapter 23

Isabella, Aniru and Chidinma arrived in Fargo to a vicious cross-wind. Most visitors to Fargo were greeted by wind before they landed. This was ground zero. And that being the case, this was where the containment had to begin, and hopefully, they would be able to discover the source of the outbreak and ultimately how it had occurred. As they made their way from the airport, Isabella and Aniru discussed how none of what was said at Camp David made any sense.

"Prokiv was describing a scenario that has no nucleus. It has no core to draw from, to go out to a set of concentric parameters and then work your way back again to find the cause," Isabella pondered.

"Everything they talked about, when you extract their ethnocidic racism, is like they are trying to find whatever strings that *seem* to be dangling and then tying them together to make a tapestry of cause and effect," Aniru followed. "But, and I think you agree, there is something else at play here that we or anyone else have no idea what the hell it is. Let's get a hotel where we can work from. Then find Dr. Amaechi's place."

Chidinma was curious about Aniru. He was from Africa; he understood her native language and he was black. Aniru and her mother also were *obviously* very close. Chidinma had seen her mother with other men periodically, but they always seemed more like acquaintances, and not at all like she acted around this man. He also didn't act like the men she had casually met, always casually, who sometimes came to take her mother here and there, treating her, when she had been introduced to them, as a novelty. Isabella had never shown any interest in those men, in fact they bored her. Aniru was different, not only could they talk to each other in their native tongues, it

70

was obvious he and her mother were together in a way that she had never seen before.

Dr. Amaechi's apartment was in West Fargo, known for welcoming the differences in people rather than shunning them. It wasn't difficult to find his name and address, simply being listed in the local directory. When Aniru and Isabella arrived, they found that Dr. Amaechi's apartment was on the third floor of the building, with a stairwell nestled in-between two of the buildings. Isabella went to the manager's office and found a young woman sitting behind a desk, vacantly sorting keys. "Hello, I am Dr. Isabella Kitchen, from the CDC," at that point showing the woman her CDC/Epidemic Intelligence Service identification. "I need to gain access to one of your tenant's apartments." The woman seemed to be befuddled at the request and said, "What is the CDC? I gotta know what it is, 'cause I have to call my manager...

"Look, I don't have a lot of time to waste on you going from person to person to get some kind of permission, I need access to an apartment now, so why don't you just bypass your manager and call either the sheriff's office or the local FBI office." Then Isabella put her ID back in her shoulder bag and waited for a response from the impertinent young woman, who then said, in an exasperated tone, "Whose apartment do you need to get into?" To which Isabella said, "Dr. Khalid Amaechi, he is on the third floor of building number three." The woman pulled a book from her desk, found Dr. Amaechi's key number, walked to a lock box on the wall and retrieved the pass key, then she began to walk out the door, indicating for Isabella to follow her.

"Hand me the key," Isabella said, "...this matter is none of your concern. I will return the key when we are done examining the apartment." Disgruntled, the young woman handed over the key and returned to her desk.

Aniru was waiting at the door of the apartment. Isabella unlocked the door. Dr. Amaechi's apartment was spartan. It struck Isabella and Aniru how everything seemed strictly utilitarian. The sofa was well-worn, and thread bare in places. There was a television, radio and two bookcases bulging with books and journals on microbiology and virology. The bathroom contained the usual shampoo and razor while the bedroom was furnished with a bed with no headboard, a side table, lamp and a closet with nothing exceptional inside. Aniru and Isabella went back to the bookcase. Pulling down books with obvious markers and quickly reviewing them for clues provided them with nothing, until Isabella found a note slipped into a copy of *The Journal of Virology Archives*. Across the piece of paper was written, "What happened in the lab today?" It was dated less than four weeks ago. It wasn't signed by anyone. Just the cryptic question. Aniru read the note, "Okay, let's assume for a minute that *clearly* something happened that exposed Dr. Amaechi to the virus. We still have no idea how it became activated."

It was then Aniru said, "Let's take one last look around." Going from one room to another they looked for anything that looked out of place. Aniru found a folder of receipts that he thought may be useful. Finally, as they were heading to the front door, Isabella quickly took a pair of surgical gloves from her pocket and said, "Shit, wait...!" Going from room to room she gathered up six metal back scratchers. She held them out to Aniru and said, "What the hell did he need these for?"

"Look closely at them," Aniru said, "They still have skin scrapings on them." Isabella dropped them in a biohazard bag as they walked out the door.

In the parking lot of the apartment building stood the young girl and a local deputy sheriff. As Aniru and Isabella came from under the breezeway between the two apartment buildings, the girl began pointing. The sheriff's deputy began walking toward Isabella and Aniru. Isabella stopped. "Officer, can I ask you what exactly you want?"

"This lady here," he said, pointing back to the office girl, "...phoned into our office, and I need to see some identification."

Isabella reached and again pulled out her CDC/Epidemic Intelligence Service identification, saying, "You can come close enough to read my ID, but you may *not* approach any closer."

"Lady I need to know what the hell you are doing here." The deputy, hanging his thumbs over his Second Place Rodeo Champion, tarnished silver belt buckle partially hidden by his now rotund swaying abdomen, began walking forward.

"Stop!" Isabella said, holding up her hand, "that is close enough."

Aniru spoke up, "Sir, should you come any closer you could contract a disease for which there is *no* cure or treatment, and you *will* die, so I suggest you stop where you are."

Isabella said, "If you have questions call the FBI field office in Fargo and then be on your way."

The deputy stood back on his heels, turned around to the still pointing and now pissed off girl, and said, "Miss, just get on back inside…"

Isabella still had her surgical gloves on when she walked to their car, opened the trunk, and put the biohazard bag in a cooler. "Okay officer, we will be leaving now, I suggest you make that phone call and then just go back on patrol."

The deputy sheriff walked back to his cruiser and pulled out of the parking lot. Aniru nor Isabella could see his eyes looking back in his rearview mirror. The office girl was frantically waving her hands and mouthing something or other as she went back to where she had come from. Isabella and Aniru got into their car and drove away, not bothering to return the key to Dr. Amaechi's apartment.

❧

# Chapter 24

ISABELLA HAD SENT THE back scratchers to the CDC for a stat BSL-4 lab analysis. It had been dispatched from the Fargo airport to Minot AFB and then to Atlanta, where it was met by a secured transport from the CDC. The analysis was classified Top Secret and the results were hand delivered to Dr. Foege, who immediately called Isabella at the motel.

"We have the results from the samples you sent. They were all positive for Marburg, Zaire Ebola and Measles."

"So, whenever the viruses became active clearly had to have occurred, after he left Dugway, obviously," Isabella said.

"Yes, we surmised as much, but the question is, as you are aware, *how* did the viruses become activated?"

"I wonder at what point in whatever discomfort Dr. Amaechi was in, did he realize that the viruses had become activated?"

"Dr. Conteh and I are going to begin tracing Dr. Amaechi steps as much as we can, we did find a financial folder in his apartment that had about a month's worth of receipts, so we are going to backtrack and see if those lead anywhere, we will contact you when we have more information."

Isabella and Aniru knew the time from incubation to fulminant onset for the virus was short. It had been just over a week since they were both drawn into this nightmare scenario. They calculated that Dr. Amaechi had been infected approximately three days prior. Looking back at the receipts they discarded all but those of the past thirteen days.

It seemed that for a man with little personal possessions he had done an inordinate amount of shopping the past month. Dr. Amaechi also appeared to always eat his meals out, most especially at an African restaurant that he frequented multiple times per week, according to the receipts always having the same thing, Jabaati/w/beans. Since he had gone to the African restaurant regularly, Aniru and Isabella thought this would be a good place to begin.

It was early evening when Isabella, Aniru and Chidinma walked into the restaurant. Other than one older couple sitting in the corner, they were the only ones now wanting to be seated. A tall man with a thick African accent looked at Aniru and said, "*Jambo*," to which Aniru said, "*Salama*." He then gracefully directed them to a table, closest to the swinging doors of the kitchen. Chidinma leaned her head back and inhaled, looked at Isabella, and said, "Mother, *what* fragrances!" Isabella reached out and pulled Chidinma close to her, while Aniru pulled out Isabella and Chidinma's chairs. When the waiter presented the menus, Aniru said that they had heard so much about the jabaati w beans that was what they would all have. "Ah... *Kikomando!*" the waiter replied, with a pleasantry of spirit. In a short while, their food was brought to the table. The jabaati was rolled and served in a halfmoon around the edge of the bowl. Chidinma was basking in the wafting aroma arising from her crock. After their meal the waiter presented them with a basket of steaming mandazi, and as Aniru commented, "Right from the fryer..."

Shortly the waiter brought the check. Isabella paid and then Aniru asked the waiter if he recognized the photo of Dr. Amaechi that Dr. Prokiv had given them. The waiter took a step back and then began to speak, "He come here many times, gets what you got, a good man, always respectful, sat over there, until a few weeks ago, when the *Popobawa* came, never came back again."

Isabella didn't know the word, but Aniru and Chidinma did. It clearly made Chidinma uncomfortable. Chidinma, now a woman of science, having just having completed her residency in infectious diseases and a post doc in tropical medicine, surprisingly still reeled when she heard of a Popobawa having been manifest at the restaurant.

Aniru, curious, asked the waiter how the Popobawa made himself known. Then the waiter told them what had happened when the Popobawa came to the restaurant.

"The man who lives in the picture sat always over there. He come here many times, as I say, very nice, not everyone is very nice, they treat you like waste people. He always orders the jabaati w beans, we bring him more jabaati because he likes to fold them to clean the bowl. The man reads, eats and reads, eats and reads, never bothers no one... A few weeks ago, the man from the table came in, ordered his jabaati w beans and then started reading. A while later another man, the Popobawa, came in."

"How was he dressed?" Aniru asked.

"He, short, very short, had a busy coat on..." Isabella asked what a busy coat was. "Like he go to work in a busy coat." Isabella assumed he meant a sport jacket. "I sit him down and he wants pancakes. I tell him we do not have such things to eat. He become very upset. Say no more, no more... *Then*, he shows his true form and the Popobawa comes out of him... The man reading and eating falls on the floor, screaming, itching, trying to get bad scratch to stop the itch, but it was all over him. Then I fall and am being eaten like by siafu too... then my cook, he come out and start screaming, arms moving his hands, he like being eaten alive by siafu... He had dreams of snakes and crows the night before the Popobawa came. My cook knew, his dream, maandamano..." Again, Isabella asked what maandamano meant. This time Chidinma said, "The cooks dream foretold the Popobawa's coming..."

"The read and eat man was crying... brushing them away... The Popobawa, he *laughing, laughing*, 'never again, never again,' he says... Then he gets up and leaves... and the curse goes with him, like smoke out the door, because the siafu stop biting."

Aniru placed his hand on Chidinma's shoulder, and speaking slowly, said to her, "I understand how the old ways can come back to us, sometimes haunting us from within, they may never completely leave us, now though, we can use what we *know* to be *real* to temper the old ways when they appear and frighten us." Chidinma reached up and placed her hand on Aniru's, nodding her head as he spoke to her.

Isabella watched as Aniru touched Chidinma's shoulder. He did not have to do this, she thought. It was an act of loving by a man who had so recently just met her daughter. Aniru could have just as easily said nothing, but he didn't, he, in that moment, put everything aside, stepped outside of himself and provide a bridge of comfort to Chidinma. In Chidinma's village, the Popobawa was not a myth, but whether called the Popobawa or another name, it brought forth, for her, the evil vapors or juju of the *Shetani*. Even though Chidinma was now well educated and had been cultured to another way of being, the old ways of her village still lived deep inside her. Aniru had immediately seen this. When his hand had touched Chidinma's shoulder, she in return placed hers on top of his. It was in this moment, beyond what they had pledged to each other, that Isabella found the depth of her love for Aniru.

After they left the restaurant Isabella and Aniru believed they had found the source of how the virus was being activated. But it didn't seem as though Dr. Amaechi had been targeted by what they were now calling the Popobawa, as it was the only name they knew. "Good God, could it be a coincidence?" Isabella said to no one really. The implication that this was nothing more than a chance encounter between the developer of the deadliest virus on earth and someone who could activate that virus, with what amounted to high frequency code, was *null*. It simply *couldn't* happen! And yet it appeared to have defied all probabilities and in fact did. Now the question was for Aniru, Isabella and Chidinma, was who the hell is the Popobawa?

After they left the restaurant, Chidinma clung close to Aniru. As they walked, he put his arm around her shoulder. Later he said, "When I was a boy the Popobawa came to my village. He too came in the form of a dream one night. Everyone in the village had the same dream, and... we were afraid. We dreamed that we were going to be eaten by a pride of hungry lions. They were coming for our village, and in our dream the men of the village took all of the children and tied them to trees so the lion could feed on us while the rest of the village could escape. The men took us out, they were many of us and tied us naked to the trees surrounding the village. The men and the women of the village abandoned us. We were frightened, crying, very upset. They never came back for us. We were tied to the trees for three days. Then on the morning of the third day, we heard rustling in the forest. We thought the Popobawa had sent the lions... But breaking through the brush were missionaries. There was no one left in the village to be saved except for the many children. A man named Reverend Elmer Burrell cut my ropes, and as fate would have it, he cared for me and raised me as one of his own. Had the Popobawa not come to our dreams that night, I would never have had the opportunities that I have had. And because the Popobawa appeared in

77

the restaurant to Dr. Amaechi that night, then we might have never known how dangerous what the doctor had made could be. Yes, it has been a tragedy and many people have died, but your mother and I, and now you also, are going to stop this." Chidinma listened and discovered that she and Aniru had come from similar circumstances. Both being saved from danger by someone who through fate or luck brought them together.

Isabella had never known anyone like Aniru. In him there was no need to defend, to be foolishly competitive and he certainly wasn't power mad or tried to shove his beliefs down someone else's throat. She could see for the first time in her life the three of them becoming a family.

Chidinma looked at Isabella and Aniru, then asked, "Will Aniru be with us after we find the Popobawa?" Isabella and Aniru looked at each other. "Chidinma, I have always included you in our lives together and I am going to do that now. I have fallen in love with Aniru and he with me. Yes, it has been very quick, and some will say, too quick. I have been close to other men but, and especially as I see the two of you together, and yes, we don't know how it will be, but yes, Aniru, I and you will be together long after we have found the Popobawa. Is that okay with you, sweetheart?" Chidinma suddenly became tearful, as she nodded her head and said, "Yes!"

# Chapter 25

ROBERT IMAGINED HE WAS now six feet four and 240 pounds. A full head of wavy hair and tightly curled chest locks teasing from his open collar sprouted from his hardened pectoralis muscles and a deep resonate voice. He looked in the smoky dreg mirror in the bath of the cheap motel. *If,* only it was true. But, even if not, Robert had *finally* known what it must be like to be a mighty oak. Having endured storm after storm, throughout many years, without bending or breaking.

For Robert, the allure was also that no one knew where his *power* was coming from. That became clear to him when he brought the insolent bus driver to his knees. And now, the patrons of the restaurant, thrashing around on the floor. One of them screaming, *Popobawa, Popobawa.* Whatever that meant, he said to himself. His prototype was a success. But he also knew that if it were to have the kind of success he had hoped for it would need to be miniaturized. It had also come to mind, after seeing the effect it had, that there may be more to the GDRP than just a toy for boys. Robert had not realized how destabilizing it could be. Imagining the GDRP on the battlefield or police armed with a GDRP. Bringing the enemy to their *knees* without firing a shot. Then, simply rounding them up or... killing them, as the case may be.

# Chapter 26

WHEN ISABELLA WAS A child her mother used to play what she called *chances are* with her. It was her way of getting Isabella to consider possibilities of things occurring and of not occurring. When she entered medical school, the *chances are* game allowed her to think about problems presented to her differently than the other students. Isabella became masterful at creating order out of something that appeared to *have* to be one way but in fact had *nothing* to do with what it appeared to be. And so a brilliant diagnostician she became.

When she had contacted Dr. Prokiv after the encounter at the restaurant, he said they were investigating threats to members of the Dugway development group. Those scientists who had been working along with Dr. Amaechi in the design of the virus. To Isabella, this didn't seem to be fertile. In the proposal Dr. Prokiv was putting forth someone would have had to know that Dr. Amaechi had been exposed to the virus and then to have some mechanism to activate the virus. This had far too many mechanisms completely dependent upon the other for it to succeed. Plus, any failure, of any step in the process, would likely nullify any progress in the investigation so far. To Isabella, regardless of to how it appeared, the encounter with the Popobawa seemed entirely random and coincidental. As she went over the conversation with Dr. Prokiv, Isabella looked at Aniru and said, "We are looking for an enigma. Prokiv thinks it is some kind of plot, but especially after the *Popobawa*, I don't believe he is right." Aniru agreed with Isabella, the difficulty now was how to proceed. They would have to wait until the Popobawa showed himself again.

# Chapter 27

ROBERT HAD SLEPT WELL the night before. He dressed and walked, looking for breakfast. Bobby had always loved breakfast and now with his transition to Robert, well he seemed to love it even more.

Alas, there on the corner was the Plugged Nickel. A flashing sign said *The Best Breakfast in Town.* Even in his darkest times, he did his best to make sure he had a good breakfast. Robert loved pancakes; those of course were his favorites. But, on this brisk morning, he wanted eggs, sausage and crisp hash browns, a large orange juice and black coffee. He always took his eggs scrambled, really preferring them sunny-side up but... Robert said, it bothered him the way the yolks looked back at him before he salted, peppered and ate them. And if they weren't fried just right, they wobbled and he was *not* going to eat anything that wobbled.

He could tell right away that the Plugged Nickle was going to be just right. A short order cook was slinging out orders just as fast at the waitress at the counter could call them in. When his order was set down in front of him, he thought for a moment that he just might move here, to have this breakfast every day. What a silly thought, he thought. His first fork full of the scrambled eggs was sublime, almost orange in their color, soft in his mouth. Followed by the perfect bite of sage sausage... and the hash browns tasting like the potatoes had been dug out of the ground that morning. All followed by dark coffee to wash it all down. He would save the orange juice as an after-breakfast indulgence for eating so well and heartily.

At one of three tables against the window sat a man with an unbecoming beard across from a woman with the well-worn look of having lived too long on the dusty road of dejection.

"Stupid cunt..." he said to her in a voice that assured everyone could hear. The woman, whose chin looked permanently affixed to her chest, had tears running down her cheeks. The bearded bastard looked up at the waitress, "She's so fucking stupid, this is what I have to put up with, day after fucking day..." Robert sat and watched for a moment. Just a few days ago, he could have done nothing except skulk out the door. But today...

Robert picked up this briefcase, walked over to the table and sat down in the chair beside the woman. The man looked at Robert, bewildered. Then suddenly the man began to itch. It started out innocuously, him reaching around to his back, his fingers going down his shirt, trying to reach that damn spot. But, then, with his arm still contorted, it was as though he was on fire. His arms couldn't move fast enough, trying to get to everywhere he was itching. The fire ants had come again. He became so out of control he fell out of his chair and onto the floor. "Jesus, make it stop... make it stop..."

Then Robert let up on the button that activated the GDRP. The bastard, gasping like there was no air to breathe, just as suddenly as he had started, stopped itching. Robert looked at him, "Apologize to this lady..." he said to the man.

"Fuck you..." the man said, seeming not to have learned his lesson.

Robert held the button down again and the man immediately began itching and scratching. "I'm sorry, Jesus Christ, I'm sorry..."

"Good," Robert said. "Give me your wallet." Sheepishly, the man pulled his wallet from his back pocket and still laying on the floor handed it to Robert. Robert took the wallet, pulled out the man's driver's license and put it into his pocket. "I know where to find you now... Think about me before you start up again... next time I won't stop, and you will die of heart failure." Then Robert collected himself, paid for his wonderful breakfast and walked out the door. The other patrons of the restaurant began applauding Robert. Not a one was singing, "Five foot two, A little chunky with eyes of blue, there goes Little Bobby in his unmatched shoes.... won't anybody be his pal...?"

# Chapter 28

Isabella, Aniru and Chidinma had spent the day trying to figure out how they could track down the Popobawa. Yet in all of their figuring nothing had come to mind that they believed would bear any results. As they looked back at the original sighting of the Popobawa at the restaurant, it seemed as though he had entered the restaurant wanting something that the restaurant did not serve. From the description, it didn't appear that he had come in looking to cause havoc, but once he was told that he couldn't have what he wanted he became enraged and that was when the Popobawa emerged. But... the question about who he was was one thing but how had he caused what Aniru said sounded like some extreme histamine response, was something else entirely.

How could someone cause a histamine response in someone else? The Popobawa wasn't touching the man, and in fact was sitting at least twenty feet away from Dr. Amaechi when he began to react to something the Popobawa was doing. Chidinma sat listening to Aniru and Isabella talk about the Popobawa, when she spoke up and said, "It's like he is casting a spell..." Then there was momentary silence. Isabella and Aniru looked at each other. Then it came together. They had been thinking only scientifically, but in fact he had to be casting a spell. But, what had he been using as his scepter?

Aniru thought out loud, "According to the gentleman we talked to at the restaurant, the Popobawa became angry when the server wasn't able to prepare him pancakes. And then he held up his briefcase, that's it, there must have been something in the briefcase. Because the server said 'he pointed the case he had with him at me...' *If* there was some kind of device in that case that could produce UHF waves that could create a severe histamine response and inadvertently was the frequency that would activate the virus... The chances of the Popobawa knowing that Dr. Amaechi would be there, much less that he was a scientist who had developed this scourge of a bioweapon, is astronomical."

Isabella added, "Plus, it doesn't sound like he pointed the case directly at Dr. Amaechi, he got hit with whatever kind of electronic *spell*, to use Chidinma's word, he generated from inside the briefcase."

Aniru continued, "And when the cook came out from the kitchen, it sounds like he walked into the electromagnetic spectrum and reacted exactly like the owner and Dr. Amaechi. But, Dr. Amaechi was *nothing* more than a random bystander."

Dear God, calculate those odds. So, whoever Dr. Amaechi came in contact with after the Popobawa activated the virus has to be either now dead or close to death. But why haven't we heard something? When someone presents to an ER with these symptoms, they would *have* to go into lockdown." Isabella spoke with the inflection of a question, silently hoping there would be a previously unheard voice with a definitive answer.

"There may be another way to approach this," Aniru said. "Let assume for a moment that Dr. Amaechi was the only one from Dugway who was exposed, however. Before he encountered the Popobawa the virus had remained inert. There was no way, they assumed, for the virus to become activated because the UHF/EHF were coded in such a way that they believed it couldn't be replicated outside of the lab, so Dr. Amaechi likely did not even know he was even infected until the symptoms overwhelmed his disbelief. Once he did realize that the activation had occurred was when he wrote the message we found. He just couldn't figure out how the monster he had created had been struck by lightning and come alive. So, we know now that someone, by some inexplicable way, has created some kind of device that replicates the UHF code that activates the virus. But... a remaining question and certainly of equal, and maybe of greater importance, is whether or not whoever this person is—have they also stumbled on the EHF frequency that deactivates this goddamn scourge."

# Chapter 29

DPG is eight hundred thousand acres. Signs hang on electric charged fences that read, "*Warning: Restricted Area, Use of Deadly Force Authorized*." In 1969 the development of all biological weapons was ordered halted, and the stockpiles destroyed. But a *defensive* program was also ordered continued. Defensive operations are easily reverse-engineered to make a *cure* an apocalyptic *menace*. The scientists who had worked on the 666 Project with Dr. Amaechi numbered no more than six. When they met collectively, after being interrogated by military intelligence, there was terror amongst themselves. They lacked not only any knowledge of an accidental exposure they also were confounded how such a leak could have occurred. They were also on lockdown confinement at DPG. Dr. Amaechi was tireless in his dedication to following BSL-4 safety requirements, as were all of the scientists working on the project.

It was not long after the last meeting with the interrogators that Dr. May Ying, who officially was from the Biological Test Division at WDTC/DPG, voiced a thought that no one had considered. Not only from the standpoint of 'you always trust your equipment,' but also because the thought was terrifying. Sitting among the others, Dr. Ying looked around the room and then said, "What if we are looking at this the wrong way?" The other scientists looked inquisitive. "We developed the virus, we knew its nm size, we all took standard protocol BSL-4 precautions, we all decom'd when we exited the lab, we were always paired, so no one could have obtained a sample of the virus... But... what if the virus, because of the recombinant nature of it being a manufactured tri-part pathogen, when it was engineered, actually became so many nm's smaller that it penetrated our protective gear? Our suits are 20 mil thick, so the virus would have to have recombined into likely a negative size for it to be able to penetrate the suits pores. Nothing, absolutely nothing, is 100% solid, even with positive pressure... This is an *unthinkable* consideration, but we need to measure the virus' recom'd size. And, if this is the case, it means we are all infected, no matter what our blood tests show. We simply haven't been exposed to the respective frequency to activate the virus."

Another scientist involved in the project spoke up, "What you are saying makes no sense, and I am surprised that you are raising this as a consideration, *and* we are in completely unknown territory, *and* I agree we have to review the virus' size. I also want to say that, if this has happened, then not only have we created a potentially *unstoppable monster*, but we have also completely redefined viral research and understanding for all time."

Dr. Ying, before they embarked on their now mission to determine 666's size, suggested that the group review the video of all of Dr. Amaechi's entrance and exits one week before he left DPG for good. The group discovered that he had only entered BSL-4 one time. He was only inside for thirty-three minutes, from suiting up to his exit. After his exit he called a meeting with the development group and then left DPG, never to return. One of the scientists carried a portable viewer of Dr. Amaechi's time in and out of the facility. Dr. Ying volunteered to be the one and the only one who would enter the lab. The scientist with the recording directed her through the exact same steps and procedures that Dr. Amaechi had gone through on his final entrance to BSL-4. When Dr. Ying was finalizing her suiting up, she took a roll of ordinary refrigeration tape and began wrapping it around the cuff of her surgical gloves, four times. Dr. Ying then began to secure her footing in the rubber boots attached to her suit, when the scientist directing her from the video tape said, "Wait... Dr. Ying, we have a problem. You, per protocol, glove wrapped four times. In the surveillance video, Dr. Amaechi only did one turn of the tape around his wrist." They both zoomed in on that section of tape and also saw that not only did Dr. Amaechi only make one turn of the tape around the cuff of his gloves, but the ends of the tape did also not overlap, leaving a minuscule breach at the cuff of his glove. Dr. Ying continued to suit up according to protocol. When she entered BSL-4 she did everything that she was directed to do by the scientist monitoring the video of Dr. Amaechi actions and movements. He had done nothing out of protocol other than fail to fully glove wrap and enter the BSL-4 alone. To the undiscerning eye, this would be understood to be of little importance but... When Dr. Ying completed the repetitious movements of Dr. Amaechi, she took a sample of the 666 and measured the virus' nm size. The other scientists heard her through the com say, "Fuck..." She then exited BSL-4, decontaminated, and met with the others. When she entered the conference room she said, "We have found the source and reason for the leak."

"Dr. Amaechi failed to follow protocol." "He, as we ascertained from the video, only glove wrapped one time and even with that failure, he violated protocol secondarily by not end-to-end over-lapping of the refrigeration tape. However, when I measured the virus size, I have discovered that it appears, as I really have no other microbiological explanation, that once the independent viral entities were combined a metamorphosis of some type occurred in the final combinatoric virus, which resulted in it reducing its size to a < 0 nm. Clearly, I *know* this cannot be, however, it does not change the fact that it is. What we have then is a virus that has a lethality of 100%, and no physical barriers that would prevent its ability to breach that barrier. In other words, our PPEs provide little if any security." Dr. Amaechi was compromised by both his own failure to follow protocol and by the metamorphoses of the viral size. Avoiding exposure in its presence would only be a matter of *luck*, plain goddamn luck, and nothing more." Dr. Ying thought to herself, "Jesus... if this thing ever gets a foothold... what have I become a part of?"

Dr. Amaechi was the Chief of the division, he was a virologist with over two hundred publications to his name and he was sought after by the most esteemed universities in the world, yet he chose to remain with the WDTC/DPG. It just didn't make any kind of logical sense that he would enter a BSL-4 and only glove wrap one time and then not even overlapping the ends of the tape. He was the chief designer of the 666 Virus, he knew its level of lethality. And yet... Dr. Amaechi clearly failed to follow safety guidelines. In observing the surveillance video, his failure, Dr. Ying thought, 'was also sloppy, reckless.' A BSL-4 is not the type of enclosure where you can, euphemistically, *'run in and out.'* Any in and out requires a rigidly defined safety protocol.

Dr. Ying, keeping her thoughts to herself, wondered what motivation might Dr. Amaechi might have—for potentially anyway—deliberately exposing himself to the virus. What could he possibly gain that would be worth the risk of setting the most lethal virus ever known to man run rampant? In sequence of events, it was shortly after Dr. Ying had reported her groups findings that Dr. Prokiv called Isabella.

People like and even demand answers for everything. They become restless when those answers are impossible to be found.

# Chapter 30

Isabella answered the phone in the motel. It was Dr. Prokiv. "Dr. Kitchen, this is Dr. Prokiv, we have just received word from the Dugway Group, and they believe they have discovered how the breach occurred. I won't go into details, but suffice to say, there is no ongoing threat and after discussing the situation with the President and Dr. Foege, we collectively believe the crisis is over and you and Dr. Conteh are hereby ordered to stand down. Your country of course thanks you for what you have done, but your services are no longer required regarding this situation. Dr. Foege has suggested you take a few days and report back to the CDC, assuming your normal duties at the beginning of next week. Please extend our appreciation to Dr. Conteh for his service." And on that final note, Dr. Prokiv terminated the call.

Isabella looked at Aniru, "We've been fired..." Aniru looked inquisitively. Then Isabella told him as Chidinma listened also. "This makes no sense," he said, adding, "The Popobawa is still out there."

"Dr. Prokiv wouldn't reveal how the breach at DPG occurred, but he said we were no longer needed. I was told to report back to the CDC at the beginning of next week. Prokiv sounded like he was calling his wife to tell her not to forget to get eggs! There was *no* emotion whatsoever. And the perfunctory *thank you*... Oh, he said to thank you also..."

Aniru spoke up and said, "That's comforting, there is something wrong here, the Popobawa is still unidentified, as we know it anyway, we haven't been told how the virus was leaked, and we cannot be sure that somehow there are others who have been infected. It concerns me that if the Popobawa has, for whatever reason, and unbeknownst to him, cracked the code for the frequency activation of 666, then it clearly means others, if they are set on doing so, can crack it also. Even if we stop looking for the Popobawa, this is far from over, reduced in its immediacy, yes, but not over... They know something that we don't, or they have another agenda that we are not privy too."

They all felt a conflict between relief and foreboding. Each looked at the other. Aniru and Isabella looked at each other, never having had the opportunity to talk about what happens to them once this is over. And now the answer that remained to be answered was thrust upon them. Isabella then spoke up, "Like I said, when we were at Camp David, I am resigning from the CDC. I am a doctor and a scientist, I am *not* a fucking politician, and after this and what we have seen, I won't be a part of this any longer."

"Isabella, I was in the States to do a series of lectures on infectious diseases in rural settings, training docs what to look for, then..." Aniru said. "The clinic I was working at in Sierra Leone has closed. I am a doctor without a country..."

To which Isabella said, "You are also the world's foremost expert on Lassa Fever... Perhaps we could both get a professorship and do consultations on tropical diseases."

"Atlanta is one of the busiest hubs for international travel..." Then, Isabella and Aniru looked at Chidinma and almost at the same time, as though they were one voice said, "How would you feel if we lived together?" Chidinma began softly crying and simply nodded, yes. She was unsure where she was going to work. Chidinma had received prestigious offers, and it was now a matter of choosing.

Isabella wrote a letter of resignation to the CDC and took a month to transfer her responsibilities. She met with Dr. Foege who asked her to reconsider her decision to resign, promising her further advancement, to which she simply said, "No." Both she and Aniru were immediately offered associate professorships at the medical school, focusing on epidemiology and tropical and rare diseases. They purchased ten acres outside of Atlanta and began growing their own food, as much as possible, anyway. Chidinma took an assistant professorship, teaching medical and doctoral students.

Both courses Isabella and Aniru taught were some of the most sought-after courses in the curriculum. If they weren't teaching, it seemed they were consulting with someone, somewhere in the world or authoring papers together. Isabella had little to do with the CDC, her clearance having been *retired* the moment her resignation was finalized. Aniru was still doing some work with other physicians and researchers in Sierra Leone and Liberia on Lassa and other hemorrhagic fevers. For many years, they had been knee-deep in blood, and they knew the fragility of life. Now that they had each other, they savoured the time they had together.

Something they had not planned for were their dogs, Henry and Acacia. Neither had ever had a so-called *pet*. But once these four-legged beings came into their lives, it was as though Isabella had just given birth. Henry developed an affinity for Aniru's pocket cap, often accompanying him when he lectured, carrying what had now become Henry's cap, in his mouth as they made their way into the lecture hall. When others stared down, Aniru would look at them and say, "Henry thought it might rain today so he insisted on bringing his cap." He never bothered to explain beyond that. Acacia, was always side-by-side with Isabella, just waiting for her to rise from her chair so she could see if Isabella had perhaps left a crumble or even dropped something she could discover and savour. Often, she would bring whatever she found and drop it onto Aniru's lap. One afternoon she found a piece of faux fur, where, God knows, but she pranced through the house with it like it was Russian sable. She also had an affinity for watching television, not a snippet here and there, but entire shows.

Until it was no longer practical Chidinma always came home for the holidays, the three of them celebrating whatever the occasion was together. Chidinma's visits were becoming increasingly rare now, demands for her time were increasing and her days began looking like weeks. On one of here last visits, the three of them were sitting together after dinner, Chidinma said, "My life has been both tragedy and wonderment." Looking at Isabella, she said, "You found me, likely on my way to meet death, my village decimated, took me in, and saved my life. You could have found me a family to go live with, but you took me to live as your own. You always made sure that I knew of my culture, you didn't try to make me a *white* girl, you never tried to straighten my hair, to rid me of my accent. But, most importantly, my mother, you loved me and gave me opportunities, a life that I couldn't even makeup. And Aniru, I have come to know and love you as my father. My dear father, you have given me a bridge to the place of my birth and what it means to have the love and guidance of a truly wise man."

As she boarded her plane, Isabella and Aniru thought it would be a while before they saw Chidinma again. Unfortunately, it wasn't as long as they had thought.

That afternoon it was a thick weathered stormy day in Atlanta as Aniru and Isabella took the subway from the airport back into downtown. They picked up their car and headed out to their farm.

# Chapter 31

ROBERT, AFTER HE WENT to Fargo to test his protype of the GDRP, had taken a bus back to Philadelphia. He'd had a good life, as he would say, since the toy company had brought the GDRP to market. It had been a wonderful success, the greatest ray gun, not only ever made, but ever conceived of.

Its demand had gone up right after a Congressional committee declared it a menace and something children should never be able to get their hands on. Which of course made every boy want one, "*Now!*"

The Study Group for Raising Healthy Children said in their report to the full congress that the *irritation* the GDRP caused was *Histamine-dependent itching*. Especially, as they said, "...because the reaction produced by exposure to the GDRP lasted as long as the person held down the trigger." There was also a second, top secret report, that examined the *concept* of the GDRP for use on the battlefield.

Robert had made vice-president, and being referred to as Little Bobby Two Shoes, well, he'd not even thought of himself like that any longer, and neither had anyone else. He had joined several organizations, and even at times had the accompany of a lady or two, and no longer lived in a row house. Although only known to Robert, there were times when he would dress in a trench coat, dark glasses and go, as he liked to call it, "hunting..." Finding those bullying others, those less fortunate, those who needed defending. On those occasions, he still took his special briefcase, which he had modified to increase the itching effects. Certain people simply needed to pay for the kinds of things they did.

## Chapter 32

THREE THOUSAND FEET INTO the depths of the Grand Canyon is the Supai Reservation. There are no roads into Supai and it is the only area in the United States that still uses a mule train to get its regular supplies. There are about 200 Indians who lived there and "Christ," Dr. Prokiv would say regularly, "They only have Havasupai Elementary School, not *even* a fucking high school, just a stupid bunch of leftover Indians." But, the Natives had done enough petitioning so that in 1975 they finally got complete control of the Res. So, given the beauty of the place, they opened it up to the tourist trade, started issuing visitation permits and hikers would show up exhausted having not appreciating the eight miles just to hike in, sometimes suffering from hyperthermia. There were only two trails that led to Supai. One was so rugged because of the heat, pits, and cragginess of the rock-strewn trail, that hikers' boots would be worn through by the time they got to Supai. The other trail was better because of the pretty regular mule train. But the wranglers, if they caught a hiker on *their* trail, would tell them to turn the fuck back. "This trail is used for Postal Delivery only, now get on the fuck out of here."

The Indians hated the visitors, but it made them what little money they had, most of them living in dire poverty. "Hell," the Elder of the Tribal Council would say, "These whites' shoes cost more than most of us here make in a whole year. They come in here with their cameras and take pictures of us like we're animals in a zoo. They want us to dress up like *Indians*, hoot and holler and act like what *real* Indians are supposed to act like."

Usually, the mule train would come a few times a week, but this particular week there hadn't been hide nor hair of it since Monday and it was now Friday. Plus, there hadn't even been any annoying hikers since several days before that. One of the Elders had tried to call from the only phone on the Reservation, but he'd guessed the lines were down, because he couldn't even hear a dial tone in his ear.

The principal at the Havasupai Elementary School, Fawn Wescogame, heard the whirling blades of the helicopter right after lunch break. It was late to hear a helicopter approaching. Fawn also served on the Tribal Council, who were always informed if there was a chopper bringing in someone, usually from the BLM or needed medical supplies. But she had heard nothing about a bird coming in today.

It hadn't sounded like the regular whirl of transport choppers that, if they were going to make their way to Supai, came in fast and low. There were 94 students enrolled at the school but, like most days, only 70 some showed up. Fawn was always worried about "her kids..." She of course knew all the families and was related to about half. Truth be told, if the kids made it through to the eighth grade, only about ten percent would go onto high school. But they had to leave the Res if they were to go to high school, the only choice being The Sherman Indian High School in Riverside, California. It was free room and board, but they only graduated about sixty-percent of the students who attended. Fawn often thought that the government treated the Indians like an untreated venereal disease, just letting them die a slow painful death, spread out over many years. Those tribes that were surviving were nothing more than *apples*, red on the outside, white on the inside. The isolated tribes were the ones suffering the worse, pathetically poor, chewed up by addiction and piss poor education, write offs.

Fawn walked outside and looked up at black helicopter, circling Supai, coming in low and then rapidly arching upward. On one pass she saw the four cylinders attached to prongs extending from the side struts, releasing a fine mist, as the chopper made pass after pass over the Reservation. It had seemed to start at the middle of the Res and then made outward concentric circles. When it reached a certain point, the helicopter made a hard right pitch and then disappeared against the surrounding mountains.

Other members of the tribe had come out and were watching the chopper's flight over Supai. A few of the children who were not inside the school waved, always getting excited when the whirly birds landed. Of course, they were disappointed that the choppers didn't come down, but were excited by the dew coming from the canisters under the struts. Fawn screamed at a couple of the younger children who were running around, holding their heads back and their mouths open, trying to catch some of the misty concentrate.

When Fawn looked up at the chopper, she noticed how odd the pilot seemed to be dressed, "He looks like he should be spraying for cockroaches, not flying a helicopter..." she said out loud to no one in particular.

It was several days later, no one, if there had been anyone left, could have remembered, when the second helicopter arrived in Supai. It didn't land either.

The children who weren't in school ran outside again to see the whirling blades of the chopper. Fawn continued to be bewildered as did other members of the Tribal Council and were increasingly frustrated at not being able to call out. The day before, one of the young men of the village, who knew the mountainous area around Supai, had gone over top of Havasu Canyon and saw dozens of Army vehicles parked around the perimeter. Soldiers were outside their vehicles, patrolling, armed. When he returned and told the Council, they too were bewildered. One of the Elders told him to go back over the mountain to watch what the white soldiers were doing and to come back and inform the Council. If they were up to something the Council needed to know.

The circling helicopter made several passes over Supai, and then seemed to angle about forty degrees down pitch, heading toward the center of the village. Then... the itching started. Fawn fell to the ground, her hands clawing anywhere her fingers could reach, she felt as though she had been stripped naked, and suspended into a vat of fire ants, who were eating her alive. The children who were outside too were falling to the ground, itching, as was ever member of the tribe, whether they were outside or inside thinking they were safe. The chopper hovered for five minutes or so and then made a few circles around the village proper, before it raised its pitch and flew away. Immediately after its nose lifted, and began its ascension, the horrific itching stopped. The Indians lay exhausted on the dusty ground or in their shacks. Most of them were bleeding from anywhere they could scratch themselves when the itching started. Fawn and the children who had run outside seemed to be the worse, because they were right in the line of the chopper as it pointed itself at them. She didn't know what had happened. But Fawn did know that she was thankful when the itching stopped.

There had been about 30 tribal members in the Havasupai Church having Bible study, praising God. Pastor Dan, an Elder, was recovering and doing his best to tend to the wounds the scratching had inflicted. He looked to the alter and said, "Jesus, what has happened here..." Pastor Dan was afraid that the God of evil, *Hokomata*, had just descended upon the village. Many of the younger members of the tribe didn't know about Hokomata, but Pastor Dan, being much older, with a long, gray braid that hung down his back, had been told the stories of Hokomata covering the world with the plague of a great flood. As he continued to stare at the altar, blood from his clawing dripping onto the floor of the Sanctuary, he became afraid that another kind of plague had just been brought upon his village.

It was one day later, about two in the afternoon, when Fawn Wescogame stumbled out onto the playground of the school and collapsed in a stupor. She'd first began bleeding from between her legs, but she was long past her childbearing years, and the amount of blood... It wasn't long before every orifice seemed to be percolating blood with each beat of her heart. As she lolled her head to one side, she could see *her* children laying on the ground, bleeding from their eyes, nose and ears. It looked through her wetted eyes like the children had messed their pants, but then Fawn realized that their pants were soaked with blood. She looked up to the sky and said, "My God, what is happening?"

Pastor Dan and the women who had come to set up for the community supper were lying, writhing before the altar. He looked around, saying his well exercised words that he always used to give comfort to those suffering souls. The last thing that Pastor Dan was cognizant of knowing, before he blessedly lapsed into unconsciousness, preparing to cross over into death, was that instead of bringing about the plague of a great flood, that Hokomata had brought about a plague of great blood.

In three days from the visit of the helicopter hovering over Supai and releasing the torrent of UHF waves, the population of the Supai Reservation was dead. Dr. Prokiv flew over the village to survey the second kill test of the 666 virus. It had been a long while now since the first test of the African village. But like Dr. Prokiv had said about the village, "...They were dying out anyway, we just got rid of them faster than would happen if we let them die out on their own." His attitude was even more jaded about Supai. "These damn Indians have caused the Government so fucking much time and money. Jesus, they lost their land because they wanted damn blankets and trinkets, the government gave them their blankets and trinkets and they gave us a deed to the land. When I was in college I sold my roommate a car for a hundred bucks, it's worth ten times that now, maybe I should raise hell and tell him I want the other nine-hundred dollars, I *think*, he owes me. These Indians, there are only a few hundred of this bunch left. You had brother fucking sister, first cousins marrying, and on and on, pretty soon it would be nothing but a bunch of costly, genetic gomers, hell there aren't even names for some of the chromosomal oddities. Good riddance." There was no one around to hear his justifications for genocide.

Dr. Prokiv now had all of the confirmation he needed that the 666 virus and its engineered response to be activated/deactivated by UHF/EHF was, in many respects, a greater advancement in warfare than nuclear weapons. It's cleaner, far easier to control, and there is *no* infrastructure damage, that is ours for the taking... Hell, with this, entire fucking nations can be brought to their knees, and they couldn't do a goddamn thing about it, *nothing*, not *one* thing. Do what we want, or we activate the virus..." he said to no one.

Dr. Prokiv ordered the full perimeter be secured until the unit commander received further orders.

It took Dr. Prokiv's chopper three hours to reach Dugway, arriving just a few minutes after Air Force One had set down. Dr. Prokiv was ushered to an isolated SCIF to meet with the President directly. "Mr. President, I can confirm that the second, but more refined test of the 666 Virus, was a complete success. One hundred percent mortality within a 48-hour period. We now, without debate, have what is the most important military weapon since the detonation of the atomic bomb. Sir, as you are aware, of course, the United States is in violation of the Biological and Toxic Weapons Convention of 1972... however, Sir, we know that the Russians and Chinese have also been working on bioweapons so, as you Sir and the Joint Chiefs have discussed, we *must* be at the forefront of this technology, violation or not. And

Mr. President, to continue briefly, we *have* accomplished this. Once this meeting is terminated the Supai Village will be incinerated by a thermobaric Dicyanoacetylene ($C_4N_2$) thermite device, which will reach temperatures of over 9000° Fahrenheit. The Special Skills Officer in command of the CIA's Biohazard Remediation Specialists, will manage the rest of the clean-up."

"Once the public becomes aware of the dissipation of Supai, how will this be managed?" the President asked. "Sir, the Supai village, as you are aware, was chosen as it was the most inhabited, isolated contiguous area in the continental United States, with a *failure destined* native population. There have been fire threats there for many years, so the public will eventually be informed that a lightning strike set off a massive and rapidly spreading wildfire. Because of Supai's geographic isolation, fire suppression crews were not able to reach the area in time to prevent such a profound and tragic loss of life. No members of the community were able to be saved. The area is closed off because of the possibility of disease developing from bodies contaminating the Redwall-Muav aquifer, which feeds where the Supai villagers got their fresh water. I have considered *every* detail regarding the post-event questions. There will be ceremonies, etc., lauding the Supai Village, support will be offered to those few relatives outside of the village... all the usual accolades and expressed sorrows..."

"You know some fucking senator or congressman, once the discovery is made of the demise of the village, is going to be demanding an investigation of this and that bullshit," the President spoke up.

"Again, Sir, because of the background investigations you ordered on each of the members of congress, when you first came into office, should they rattle their sabers we *will* have a private meeting with them, present them with what the investigation turned up and shut them down. You have no concerns."

"Sir, respectfully, let me add," Dr. Prokiv said. "Mr. President, *you*, for all practical purposes, now control the world, should the need arise to exercise this option utilizing this technology." The President nodded and in closing added, "Thank you, Dr. Prokiv, for chairing this project and bringing it to such a monumental conclusion. One other thing, Mr. President, there is no paper on this matter, nothing to trace back *anywhere*. The Biohazard Remediation Specialists understand their assignment is to take care of the aftermath of a tragic fire, etc. There is simply *nothing* to backtrack. One other brief thing, all deliveries were shut down shortly before the *fire* because of concerns to the public, all Tribal permits into Supai were intercepted before they could be delivered, and all postal delivery was also terminated prior to the fire. By the way, Sir, were you aware Supai was the only sector in the United States that still relied on mules for postal services?"

The President said, "Christ these damn people were living like it was the 1800s..."

It was shortly after Dr. Prokiv left Dugway and the President had boarded AF1 that a small CIA designated fighter jet flew in at just over 500 feet above Supai and released the thermobaric explosive device, and then rapidly pulled up at more than 7gs to escape the vacuum shock of the explosion. Two seconds later, the Supai Village and all of its former inhabitants vanished in an unearthly, incinerating... *whoosh*.

The young man, Armando Sinyella, who had gone over the mountain to see what the white man was conniving, came back to Supai two days after its incineration. When he came to the top of the mountain, looking down on the village, he cleared his eyes of the dust raised by his boots, then he looked up towards the familiar surrounding cliffs to make sure that, somehow, he hadn't gotten disoriented from the heat. Armando then descended into hell. Supai was now but winds swept dunes of ash that looked like burnt snow. He wondered if he was dead. It was hard to tell where he was in his village that once was, everything was the same, now only the huffing of an angry God stirred the ash. As Armando made his way here and there, he noticed there were no bones, everything had been cremated. He had no words. Armando thought he may be the last person left alive on earth. He knew how to shed tears for one, for two... but for *all*, for everything, this he did not know.

# Chapter 33

COINCIDENCES ARE THOSE THINGS that happen that shouldn't, and in many circumstances those things that happen coincidentally that no one believes were in fact a coincidence.

A month or so after the Supai Village had been immolated, Robert had decided to take a drive across the western United States. He had never seen the Grand Canyon and now with his success he could afford to do so. And although his mother would have disapproved, he was in the accompaniment of Althea, whom Robert had met at the Grace Fellowship Singles Ministry Wednesday night mingle. Althea, as some folks had said, was a brute of a woman. Not wanting to let anyone get a leg up on her, and so it had been hard for her to find a man who would be able to take what was sometimes a tongue lashing that left welts on one's very soul. But the moment Robert and Althea met on that faithful Wednesday night, well, they never left one another's side. When Robert had been Little Bobby Two Shoes, he had learned to steel-up his endurance, from the day in and day out verbal tyranny of his co-workers. Now, with Althea he was able to see the world with another set of eyes, and through those other eyes he was able to grasp that perhaps anonymous revenge at having been treated so badly was like clearing a garden of noxious weeds.

# Chapter 34

FOR THE PAST MONTH or so, Armando wandered like Moses in the desert after witnessing the aftermath of the annihilation of Supai. Most of the time he had no idea where he was, but mostly Armando thought he had been displaced into the other world. He hadn't committed suicide, and he had always been a good son, so why was he being punished? This has to be the bottom of the pitch-black river, for pitch-black was all he saw. Really, though, he just saw brown snow wherever his eyes cast, mound after mound of blowing and drifting ash, of all who once were. If he was where he thought he was, then he knew he would have to spend the next four-thousand years atoning for the wrongs that he didn't know he had done.

It was a Thursday afternoon, when he walked, filthy, dehydrated and exhausted into the Peach Springs Trading Post. Armando slid along the log walls of the trading post, to hold himself up as he made his way inside. There were several whites inside who were appalled by his appearance. *Clearly*, he was a filthy drunk Indian, who Althea said, "...should be required by law to stay on their reservations." Robert nodded in agreement. Robert and Althea had been picking out genuine Indian beaded bracelets, blankets and, real miniature deer skin drums (set of three for...), to give to Althea's nieces and nephews. Robert and Althea were on their "...western excursion," as they called their trip more than once. It was here at the Peach Springs Trading Post, where they were sure they would encounter *real* Indians.

Armando's lips were swollen, cracked and dry with suppurating blisters. His tongue was so fat he couldn't talk. No one reached out to help him. Armando only wanted some water, but he was unable to speak the word. His stench also drove the disdainful away. He wasn't sure if he was of this world or the other, if he was dead or alive, although he smelled like he was dead, even to himself. For some reason or other, wherever Althea turned, Armando was there, constantly being in her way. At one point she thought he had the temerity to actually fall into her, causing her to drop her gatherings onto the floor and likely fouling the freshness of her scent. "I have had *enough*," she said, calling to Robert.

Seeing what was going on, Robert went out to the car, got a leather shaving bag from the trunk, walked back inside, and pointed the shaving bag at Armando. Then Armando fell to the floor, symmetrical crimson lines opened on his arms as he clawed himself, trying to stop the itching. He was so dry that the caked dirt on his cheeks cracked like a droughted field under a blazing sun and had no voice by which to scream.

Althea had heard Robert talk about his GDRP, she had seen the toy, but she had never seen how Robert now carried the GDRP he had made only for himself. As Armando lay, writhing on the dust covered floor of the trading post, Althea watched and nodded at this filthy man, who had the audacity to do what he had done and was finally being taught a lesson. It was time someone taught these people how to behave around those who had an education and a proper upbringing. Althea had never been prouder of Robert.

In a few seconds, Robert released the activation button and the GDRP stopped emitting UHF waves. Armando lay on the floor, barely able to move, his breathing so shallow as to keep his lungs inflated and his heart beating. He rolled onto his back, with his eyes lolled up in his head, and said a short prayer, thanking the Creator that the itching had stopped. Robert and Althea were putting their purchases into the boot of the car. Once they were on their way, Althea scooted across the seat to sit very close to Robert. She had never done that before.

# Chapter 35

AN OLDER COUPLE WENT over to Armando and helped him to his feet. His eyes were glazed over and his breathing erratic. The old woman, had been behind Robert when he aimed the GDRP at Armando, she too felt as though her skin was crawling, her husband had been standing beside her and said he swore that one of his teeth cracked. The salesclerk told Armando he had caused enough trouble and she wanted him out of the store before she called the law.

As Armando was making his way out the door, a van pulled up, filled with blonde haired, bright-eyed Disciples of Jesus, armed under the protective armor of blessed evangelism. When Brother Randy leapt from the side door of the van, he began singing and clapping his hands, "...Lord, lay some souls upon my heart and love that soul through me; And may I humbly do my part to bring that soul to Thee.... " Then one after another, the eleven other Disciples stepped out of the van, joining Brother Randy in praiseful song. There were several other *livery posts* as they called them, along their way, to make a brief stop and deliver the Lord's message of love and salvation.

Leaning against the door was Armando, whom Brother Randy looked at and said, "My good man, Praise Jesus, you look like a stick with teeth... Boys, go get this man some water... Praise Jesus, that we rolled up when we did, Praise Jesus." A young man came out of the trading post with a cup of water. Brother Randy held the cup close to Armando's lips. "Easy, young man, easy..."

They sat Armando against the wall, as best he could, and he thanked them for their kindness. Then he said something about it being gone, it's not there anymore, swallowing each word right before all of it came out his mouth. Brother Randy told him they would take him with them, believing that the Lord had put this poor man in their path to use as a living testament to the grace and healing power of the Lord. After they were back on the road, brother Randy said, after God-given moisture to Armando's broken-down body, they would begin feeding him. "Praise be to the Lord Jesus Christ..." Brother Randy said, as those who had arrived at the trading post as twelve now left to continue their Holy mission as thirteen. Armando would be a living testament to show others how God could enter one's life like a visitor in the night, stirring one up from a sound sleep, shaking them, making them more awake than they had ever been.

Armando fell into a restless sleep as Brother Randy and the other Disciples began their journey to the next livery. Perhaps it was because Armando had been almost drained of life when Brother Randy came upon him or perhaps not, no one would ever know, no one would ever speculate, but by the time the van reached Oatman, Armando was becoming increasingly ill. Brother Randy and one of the Disciples had laid him across one of the van seats. A few miles before Oatman, he began moaning, burning up with fever. One of the Disciples got up and began tending to him, telling Armando that he would be okay, the Lord would see to it. Brother Randy had assured the other Disciples that God had guided the man to *that* livery, on *that* day and at *that* time, the embodiment of a sign of the Holy Trinity. It *was* He who brought the man and the Disciples together on a convergent path. "The mysterious pavé to salvation through Christ Jesus," Brother Randy said. As the tending Disciple looked down at Armando, he saw blood beginning to seep from his eyes and nose. Then Armando began to stiffen and shake uncontrollably.

Brother Randy drove around a dozen or so Burros that wandered here and there on the main street, as he made his way to the Oatman General Store. The other Disciples were hovering over Armando now, praying through their fear as blood was now coming from every ori-fice. The seizing had stopped now, and Armando lay motionless, his face contorted in excruciating pain. All the Disciples were covered in vomit, blood or piss. One told Brother Randy they should take Armando to the hospital. Brother Randy said he would have none of that and told the Disciple he was behaving like a Doubting Thomas. The Lord had placed Armando with the Disciples not only for both his physical body to be healed but for his soul to be delivered up to

Christ. In a few short minutes, as they sat in front of the General Store, Armando, jerked two or three times, and then... his heart stopped.

Brother Randy proclaimed that the Lord Jesus had taken Armando as one of his own. "In the eyes of God, this young man must have been very special indeed, for the good Lord to have put him up on the cross, and to bring us to minister to him before he raised this young man to Heaven... Praise be to God..." Brother Randy said. He then told the other Disciples to take a seat, leaned out the window and asked a gentleman opening the door of the general store where the hospital was. The man raised his arm and pointed, and said, "Just up the road..."

The van pulled up to the E.R. entrance of the Oatman General Hospital. The Disciples gathered Armando's body, and laid it on a smoking bench, sitting to the right of the automatic doors. They crossed his arms across his breasts and placed his hands over his heart. Then they reboarded the van. As they left Oatman Brother Randy began singing,

> Jesus calls us o'er the tumult
> Of our life's wild, restless sea;
> Day by day his sweet voice sounding,
> Saying, "Christian, follow me."

# Chapter 36

ON THIS DAY, THE E.R. wasn't busy, truth be told though it was rarely busy. About the only time it had more than a cold come in, was when a tourist came through the doors who had emphysema and it was being aggravated by one of the frequent dust devils that whirled down the main street. Oliver Oatman, MD, it was just by happenstance that he had the same last name as the town, was sitting at the nurse's station, when Burl Brocius, who'd been panning for gold up in the Black Mountains for more years than anyone could remember, "...even me..." Burl'd say, came through the door and said to Doc Oatman, "Y'all better come on outcheer!" Burl'd been walking by, leading his pack burro, who was strapped heavy with panning implements and dry goods, that'd hold him for the next few weeks or so, when he saw Armando, lying dead on the bench outside the E.R., clots of pooled blood had sun baked into the concrete below his body. Thick, dried blood had caked over Armando's eyes, mouth and ears, so much so that he looked like he had on a mask.

Doc Ollie and one of the nurses ran out the door and saw Armando's body, he went over and placed his fingers on Armando's neck, clearly there was no pulse. He also felt the jaw getting stiff with postmortem rigidity. His body had been laying in direct sunlight, so Doc Ollie didn't know how long he'd been there, but one thing was certain, this young man was quite dead. He went back inside and called an orderly to bring a gurney and help him load up Armando's body and wheeled it into bay number two, one of the three E.R. bays. Doc Ollie also had the nurse notify the Sheriff's office in Kingman.

He walked around Armando's body, bending down, curious what in the hell had caused so much blood. Clearly Doc Ollie wasn't going to conduct a post, but... he wanted to see the rest of Armando's body, and to look for any signs of wounds. He pulled on a pair of exam gloves, took a pair of bandage scissors, and began cutting away the sweat and blood-soaked clothes. When he pulled back Armando's shirt, Doc Ollie stepped back. His chest, his *entire* chest looked like ripe plum skin. "Jesus Christ!" Doc Ollie said. The nurse, who had gone outside with Doc Ollie, suddenly pulled back the curtain of the exam bay, when Doc Ollie screamed, "Don't come in here!" But, at the moment he heard the words leave his mouth, he realized it didn't matter, he, the nurse, the orderly and Burl had reached the end of their journey.

Doc Ollie had never seen anything like this, but he knew the man lying on the gurney in front of him had died quick and had died a horrible death. This *thing*, this fucking thing, was *hot*. *It* was alive in this man who was dead, seemingly feeding off of him, until there was nothing left. Picking up the phone, he called back the sheriff's office in Kingman and told them not to come into the E.R. when they arrived in Oatman. The sheriff was also told to find Burl, but... "...*do not* get within 25 feet of him, talk to him through a bullhorn.

"Sheriff, you won't understand this, but if Burl refuses to stay back, don't hesitate to use lethal force. He is a walking dead man, already, he doesn't know it... If you have to kill him, do it... But again... if you do, don't go near his body."

Emergency isolation procedures were put into effect. Doc Ollie pushed Armando's body into a cooler they used to hold corpses until they were collected by the undertaker. Because of the extreme ambient temperatures, the cooler had an emergency setting of – 10 degrees. It had never been used until now. Doc Ollie then called the CEO of the hospital and told him he was locking down the E.R., no one in and no one out. He was concerned, although his understanding of how it could be, that the dead man had a hemorrhagic fever.

The doctor locked the doors into the E.R. and the other two doors that led to other sections of the hospital. He didn't know how infectious this microbe was. But with the shape the body was in and the leakage of blood, urine and stool... It would be frozen in about three hours or so. The nurse and the orderly were watching and listening to Doc Ollie. After the initial calls, Doc Ollie sat down with them and told them everything was locked down and they could not leave the

E.R. The nurse asked how long the quarantine would be in effect. He looked at her and said, "Until we know what we are dealing with." What he thought though was, *until we die.*

## Chapter 37

WHEN THE CALL CAME into the CDC's Viral Special Pathogens Branch an immediate alert was sent out to all the viral branch heads. Plus, an automatic alert was sent to Dr. Foege. When he saw the alert and the description of the body lying in a freezer at Oatman Memorial Hospital, he became panic-stricken. What he was hearing sounded like the 666, and Oatman was only a hundred and twenty-five miles from Supai. But, this *couldn't* happen, Dr. Prokiv had assured the President that everything was taken care of, "...*nothing*," he said remained and there was no way to tie anything back to the Dugway project. Dr. Foege called Dr. Oatman directly and said he wanted more detail, because what he was describing, some kind of hemorrhagic fever seemed like "...he may be jumping to conclusions."

The sheriff from Kingman found Burl tugging his burro up a dirt road, mostly used by some of the old panners and miners still looking for that life changing vein, so full of gold, that a man who'd been prospecting all his life, could finally stop, take his burro, put his feet up and watch the stars under the night sky.

He pulled about thirty feet from Burl and told him he needed to turn around and start heading back to the hospital. Burl couldn't figure why the sheriff was talking at him over the loudspeaker on top of his patrol car. He turned around and started walking toward the car. The sheriff told Burl he was commanding him to "Halt, you are not to approach the patrol car." Most folks around Oatman didn't know that Burl was about as deaf as could be, that was why he always talked so loudly. He could make out that someone was talking to him, he just had one hell of a time trying to figure out what was being said. Burl liked to get close so he could try anyway, to read their lips as best he could. The sheriff got out of the patrol car and began screaming through the loudspeaker to "...get the hell back," waving at Burl to stay away. Burl kept plodding along toward the sheriff.

The sheriff unholstered his duty weapon, told Burl to halt one more time. With the wind and the dust Burl didn't hear the sheriff. Nor did he hear the report from the discharge of the sheriff's weapon, when the copper-jacketed round struck Burl in the forehead. When Burl's burro saw him go down, he started down the hill, when he got to his body, the burro just stood there refusing to move. Given what Dr. Oatman had told him, he figured he'd just put Burl out of a pretty bad misery that was going to be coming sooner rather than later. When the sheriff called in, he was told to not approach the body and to remain at the location, someone would be there within the next few hours to retrieve the body. Even though someone approaching Burl or even coming upon the area was remote, he was told that if anyone did, they were to be turned around immediately.

In exactly three hours and forty-seven minutes a helicopter landed blowing billowing dust and dirt into the air. The sheriff began walking toward the chopper, when four men dressed in biohazard gear leapt out, one carrying a body bag. Four other men jumped out the three-o'clock door and pointed automatic weapons at the sheriff. One of the soldiers held his hand up in a stop position, telling the sheriff to stand down. The soldiers escorted the sheriff back to his patrol car and told him to be on his way. Plus, he was told there would be no report filed. The dispatcher had also been notified. If there were any questions a simple, "In error..." reason would be given for the contact between the sheriff and dispatch.

When the first group of men approached Burl's body, they sprayed the area with a concentration of ethanol and sodium hypochlorite. One of the men laid out a body bag that could be hermetically sealed once Burl was placed inside. A man at the head, one in the middle and another at the feet, lifted Burl and lowered him into the bag. Then they zipped the bag closed and then heat sealed it.

Once Burl was bagged up the men transported him back to the chopper. He was loaded inside and lifted into a tank designed at Dugway for such emergencies. Once the tank was sealed it was flooded with liquid nitrogen. Within seconds, Burl's body was frozen to a consistency of fine glass. Then a 1500 Hz tone was activated. Burl's body immediately exploded into a fine powdery dust. The dust was then incinerated at a temperature of 1800 degrees. Burl's existence was declared null and void of this earth.

After Burls' remains had been handled, an ambulance with local markings exited from the back of the chopper and made its way to the hospital where Dr. Oatman, the nurse and the orderly who had helped with Armando were together in a positive pressure tent. Dr. Oatman had not told the others what he suspected and what he believed to be their fate. His concern was that they would attempt to leave the hospital and he could not allow that to happen. He also knew that he would do whatever it took to keep them there until he figured out what to do.

In a short while, the ambulance pulled up to the ER entrance. The men who had taken care of Burl's body told Dr. Oatman, the nurse and the orderly they were being taken to another hospital where they could be observed, should they become ill and receive treatment. Dr. Oatman said nothing. Whatever had killed Armando would also be killing them, it was just a matter of time. "Christ," he thought, "So this is how it ends..." He had no idea where they were being taken but he was sure it wasn't to any metropolitan hospital. He also wondered who the hell these men were and how they were notified. There was little talk and no discussion, only a cadre of orders, including an order to put on isolation suits. Once inside the ambulance they were told they would be helivac'd to the other medical facility. The nurse began to protest, saying they had no right to take her anywhere. She also said Dr. Oatman had betrayed her and the orderly. One of the men leaned down and told her she would not be coming back, nor would the doctor or the orderly. It was best if she just shut her mouth, if she didn't, he said he would give her an injection. Before they closed the doors of the ambulance, Dr. Oatman saw them bring out Armando's body, pull out a containment area under the ambulance and lift his body into it. Then the ambulance drove away. In a few minutes they saw the waiting chopper. A back ramp lowered and the ambulance drove inside. Before the helicopter blades began to rotate and the chopper took to the air, the six-man Bacterial Viral Alert Team was deployed.

# Chapter 38

"Mr. President, there is a call from Dr. Prokiv requesting the STU-III line be activated in the Situation Room." The President's secretary interrupted the President's monthly meeting with the Secretary of Defense at the insistence of Dr. Prokiv. In a few minutes the President entered the situation room and alerted his secretary to pass the call through from Dr. Prokiv. "What the hell is this about, Dr. Prokiv, I thought this matter was closed."

"Mr. President it appears the horse has gotten out of the barn, a young Indian kid from Supai had been in the activation and distribution zones, and somehow made it off of the Reservation without being detected. He made his way to the Peach Springs Trading Post, which is a good way from the Reservation proper, especially by foot. We don't know how he got there, but from the people we have talked to, he was dirty, dehydrated, but... he didn't appear to be ill. There was no sign that indicated he was infected. Then there was some kind of altercation with this kid, and a short, scanty looking man left the store and came back in with something that a couple of the other customers said he pointed at the Indian kid. The other customers in the store told the BVAT interviewers that for a minute or two the Indian just collapsed on the ground, scratching himself all over. The other people in the store were affected by it too but nowhere near to the degree the Indian kid was."

The President interrupted, "Okay, so some damn Indian kid caused an uproar in some damn trinket store. What the hell are you calling in like this on the goddamn STU line, I thought this matter was put to bed? Sir, shortly after the man initiated what we believe was a UHF device, a group from some Church of the Final Thunder,

113

do-gooders came in, saw the kid and decided to save his soul. They took the kid, piled in a van, drove away. We believe the kid started showing symptoms of the 666. From the best we can tell the kid died on the way to Oatman, where they dumped the Indian's kid's body on a bench outside the local hospital ER, covered in blood and vomit, so they also must have been covered too, and then drove away. The hospital personnel and another man, who had to be eliminated for being uncooperative, are all contained, but the van and the men inside are nowhere to be found. We are obviously doing a perimeter search. At this point we have not been able to locate them."

The President laid the receiver on the table, and began pacing, "Jesus Christ, Oh Jesus Christ..." He was unsure if he was praying for Devine intervention or begging for forgiveness for the nightmare that he feared was about to happen.

The President's first call was to the First Lady. He told her she and the two children would be leaving immediately for Cheyenne Mountain. Her concern was that a nuclear strike was eminent. The President assured her that was not the case, it was another matter, however, and she should plan on an extended stay until the situation was completely resolved, "It may be necessary for me to join you soon." He also said she would be going by AF-1, which was unusual because the President would not be on board. Cheyenne Mountain was then alerted to go into lockdown as soon as the First Lady and the President's children arrived. The mountain was to remain in lockdown until a direct order was received from the White House or the President's arrival.

When the call came in from the President, Dr. Foege was lecturing to a group of physicians and researchers on Changes in Clinical Diagnostics and Tracking Infectious Diseases. His pager came through with a simple EMR. The only time Dr. Foege was to be paged with this code was when the Oval Office was notifying the head of the CDC that he was to cease whatever he was doing and take the call, which was likely directly from the President. "What the fuck is going on, Dr. Foege?"

"I am sorry, sir; I have no idea what you are referring to." The President's rage was warped in a shroud of terror. "The 666 is loose..." the President said. "Holy Christ, what's happened..."

The President went on to inform Dr. Foege about his conversation with Dr. Prokiv. Dr. Foege, as he was hearing the details of what had been done to the Supai Village, took the phone away from his mouth and vomited on the floor beside his desk. "Jesus Christ, what have you people done, what have you done! I thought the 666 was frozen and all testing had ceased, what have you fucking people *done*! My God, if it is loose, My God... what have you done." Tears began to run down Dr. Foege's cheeks. He knew the implications. If the 666 was loose, as the President was saying, and on a *runaway*, there would be millions of deaths. This *was* the doomsday virus. The President's silence was reflected in Dr. Foege's terror and rage. Clearly the President was immediately distancing himself from what had been put in force. Dr. Foege had not been brought into the *need-to-know* clearance on the actions taken against the Supai Village. Once the 666 had been capped off, he hadn't been fully informed of Dr. Prokiv's and the President's off-the-book's bioweapons program being run out of Dugway. "Mr. President, this is devastating, if you want me involved in this matter, then Sir, you will tell me exactly what I want to know and do exactly what I say. If you do not, then I resign from this assignment effective once we terminate this call. I am a physician, I have had to sell my soul to the Devil too many times in this job and I am done. I despise you sonofabitches!"

"Dr. Foege, you are the only one besides Dr. Prokiv, I and the staff at Dugway that have knowledge of this."

"No sir," Dr. Foege interrupted, "There is also Dr. Kitchen and Dr. Conteh and they *must* be brought into this. It is not negotiable."

The President continued, "Dr. Foege, if this thing is loose, is there *any way* to contain it?"

"Mr. President, regarding my statement to you, do you understand?"

"Dr. Foege, yes sir, you can have what you need, immediately, is this goddamn this containable!"

"Mr. President, I don't know. If it is a *runaway*, then, I don't know. There is no vaccine, it is too complex of a viral structure, three different viruses, that have likely mutated by now, requiring three different vaccines, working in conjunction with each other, while at the same time competing against three separate viral entities all wanting to survive and all taking separate actions against the vaccines. The 666 was activated by UHF and then deactivated by EHF but... once it gets a foot hold, *and* that timeline for getting a foothold is becoming less and less, then the damage is done."

"Dr. Foege, you need to know that Dugway somehow, I don't understand the science, decreased the time between activation until, as Dr. Prokiv said, symptoms began to appear."

"Mr. President, that is another way of saying that the virus' propensity to locate a host cell and then to hijack that cell group for its own replication is *much* faster. Therefore, I don't see how it could then be deactivated by EHF unless the waveform was administered immediately after the virus was activated by the UHF. Christ, Mr. President, do you see what we are up against, do you actually *understand?* Mr. President, I want my family sent immediately to one of our secure locations."

"I will see to it, Dr. Foege..." the President said. Then the President followed with, "Dr. Foege, I am sorry, I am truly sorry... Let me know how you would like to proceed."

"I will call you immediately after I speak with Dr.'s Kitchen and Conteh, they have seen this thing. I will open the emergency channel alert system for you. I will be available immediately."

# Chapter 39

Aniru had just returned from Sierra Leone. There had been a Lassa Fever outbreak that had been traced back to droppings from the West African multimammate rats that had infected a load of grain. On the morning Aniru arrived home, Isabella was teaching a seminar on tuberculosis.

"*Tuberculous kills someone every twenty seconds...* How many of you have actually diagnosed a case of TB? In the southern African nation of Lesotho, you see about 660 cases per 100,000, where in the United States, you see about *2.5* per 100,000. TB *is* the deadliest disease in the world, but if you only practice in the States, you may go your entire career and never see one case. And... it is curable. It is a difficult treatment regimen, but yes, it is curable. In the earlier and mid part of the twentieth century there were TB sanitoriums. With the discovery of streptomycin in 1943, treatment of TB was revolutionized. Indeed, a substantial leap from Cod liver oil, vinegar massages, and inhaling hemlock or turpentine. But, and tragically, TB has for the most part been forgotten about, because geographically the areas it shows its ugly head the most are poor. Unless we fear that a disease will escape the topographical confines of an outbreak and come to the more civilized parts of the world, then we only seek to contain it. TB isn't very exotic like the hemorrhagic fevers. However, getting antibiotics into a desperately poor, landlocked region is difficult. There are many physical and political hurdles, so particularly in a case like TB, it is not just about medicine."

It was then that the door opened. The dean of the medical school asked Isabella if she could have a word with her. "I just received a priority call from Dr. Foege. He said he is sending a car for you. There is something going on and he needs you at the CDC immediately. He also said he wanted your husband there also."

When Isabella left the seminar, a security guard met her and told her there had been a change of plans. She was being picked up at the hospital helipad and then being flown to pick up Aniru. Isabella became suspicious that 666 had become active again.

# Chapter 40

IT WAS ABOUT 90 miles to Las Vegas. Brother Randy had arranged for a 3-day, 72 hour, nonstop, tent revival just on the outskirts of the city. "Jesus doesn't sleep, *why* should *we* do any less than Jesus?" Brother Randy told the Disciples many times over. "All day and all night, raising souls up to the Glory of the All Mighty! There will be those who will come before the alter of Christ, begging for redemption in the middle of the night, while others are being poisoned by dreams of lust." Brother Randy knew pestilence of all sorts was often disguised as something sweet, when it was the Devil's way of tethering his vileness to a sin filled soul.

As Brother Randy was waving his arms this way and that, the Disciples van was veering into one lane and then into another. But he knew that the Disciples were protected by God Himself and *"His truth shall our shield and buckler be. ... remember your Psalms Disciples,"* Brother Randy's voice rose over the moans of Disciples now burning up with fever and retching in buckets. Brother Randy too was also consumed by fever, but he knew the heat from the Burning Bush itself was alight right in their very presence. "Praise Jesus!" he said. They were about to pull up to the revival and with several hundred people pining for salvation to be upon them. And then... as he drove up to the sinful and saw their longing faces, Brother Randy said out loud, "Lord, we pray that you would grant them understanding of the truth of what sin is, and that you would bring upon them conviction of their sins and of their need for a savior. The Lord crowns the humble with salvation!"

As best they could, the Disciples left the van, leaning against the door panels, the fender and hood, themselves praying for the strength, in what they were sure was Satan's very presence, to be able to thwart him from raising up those desperate, *so* very desperate souls, who longed to be freed from the oppression of evil. As one Disciple bled out and fell to the ground in death, the crowd knew he had been struck down by Beelzebub. They lifted his sweat, vomit and blood-soaked body above their heads and prayed to the Almighty to take his soul to Heaven. The desperate had now seen with their very eyes the evil that the Devil had cast. This wretchedness now made their hunger even stronger to be shielded under the Lord's Wings.

Brother Randy was screaming, screaming with all the voice he had left, for Jesus to cleanse these people, "...cleanse them sweet Jesus, cleanse them..." who were coming face-to-face with the very malevolent wickedness of Satan. As more of the Disciples fell to the ground, each and every one was lifted to the sky, as though the crowd was offering up a sacrifice to God Himself. The desperate soaked with the blood of those Disciples who had sacrificed them-selves at the Alter of the Lord. "...There need be *no* marble alter, this *very* ground, this Holy ground, now soaked with the blood of Christ Himself, is the only *true* alter," a voice of the desperate sang out loud! Never, *never* had there been a moment in all of mankind where so many of the Lord's disciples had been struck down in front of those with anguished souls.

On that, Brother Randy, in what were to be his final words, called for those so starved for the love of the Lord, to come and bathe in the blood of the Disciples, which had been shed for *them*. It was Brother Randy's last decree before he was taken into Heaven.

A line of longing now formed. Two men took each man, woman and child who stepped forward, by the shoulders and dipped them in the consecrated liquor, just touching their foreheads to the con-gealing claret, so it would be plentiful to others, before the Lord took it into the earth.

They knew Brother Randy and the Disciples were watching down from Heaven. So many souls had been raised up to the Lord and the Lord had reached out and cleansed them of their sins. Many of the saved got back on the busses waiting to drop them here and there. Others went to the airport and flew to destinations far and wide, while some simply drove away. It took a while before some sort of emergency response came to the site of Redemption. Those tasked with solving why there were twelve exsanguinated corpses spread here and there, where a large religious revival had been, stood perplexed. One of the investigators rolled Brother Randy's body over and saw his eyes were so swollen and blood soaked that they were ready to explode. He also saw massive, red swollen splotches on his neck. It was then that he screamed for everyone to leave the area immediately. An investigator right about the same time had his local dispatch run the license plate of the Disciples van. He was looking over at the dozen bodies, when the dispatcher said she was patching through a call from the head of the CDC, "...a Dr. Foege."

# Chapter 41

Isabella and Aniru had been landed on the helipad at the back of the CDC and then taken to a SCIF. "Something is wrong, very wrong, or else *we* wouldn't be here," Isabella said. Aniru sat quiet, he too knew something had gone very wrong. His only involvement with the CDC other than Lassa Fever had been the 666. Now he and Isabella had been brought here by chopper and rushed into a SCIF.

When Dr. Foege entered he was accompanied by no one, that too was unusual. "Hello Dr. Kitchen and Dr. Conteh, there is no way of gentling into this, the 666 is lose." Aniru looked at Dr. Foege, "What have you bastards done?" Looking ashen, Dr. Foege began sobbing and said, "Dr. Conteh, I knew nothing of the events that led up to this, *nothing*, it was the President and Goddamn Prokiv, they set this in motion along with Dugway, I just found out the extent of what they had done. We were trying to contain it, but it has spiraled out of control, completely out of control. I wanted you brought in because you are the only two physicians who have ever encountered 666, and if possible, we need to figure out a way to stop it. Even the virologists at Dugway who developed it don't know what has happened. There was an Indian village, the Supai, isolated in the Grand Canyon, you can't get there except by pack mule or helicopter. They were inbreeding and dying out, Prokiv was looking for another test site for the 666 and informed the President of the Supai village. He said it was going to be extinct in a few years anyway, so the President gave to okay to test it on the village. The village was wiped out and then burned, making it look like the result of a forest fire. But then one damn Indian kid, that's the way it always is... one damn *someone* who manages to get themselves infected, and then fucking escapes.

Then he got himself to some Indian trinket trading post and somehow, *Jesus, maybe we are just being punished by God*, do you think that could be it, maybe that's it..." Dr Foege was getting more delirious as he spoke, "We think it must have been the person who broke the UHF/EHF signal codes, by Christ, the Devil, He had a hand in this, somehow He was in the store at the same time!"

Isabella and Aniru didn't know if Dr. Foege was talking about the person who had broken the codes *or* the Devil being in the trading post when the unfortunate Indian boy came in. "I mean the odds are not even calculable, but this Indian kid was dirty, exhausted, looked like death itself and approached some fucking woman saying something. She thought he was harassing her. The man who she was apparently with saw what was going on, went outside and came back in with a bag, held it out at the Indian kid and he started withering and crying on the floor. But other people in the store also experienced the UHFs and also reacted. So, whatever this man had had, a wide dispersal area. The man and the woman paid for a bunch of crap and then left. It wasn't long after that when the Indian kid began showing symptoms of the 666. And then... it wasn't long after that when a group of twelve men, who we now know called themselves the Disciples, came in, found the Indian kid, who was getting sicker by the minute, and fucking took him with them.

"The Indian kid must have died along the way, because they dumped his body on a bench outside of the hospital in Oatman, Arizona. We also found out that an old prospector who comes out of the hills ever so often to get supplies found the body and told the ER staff. An ER doctor, a nurse and an orderly took the Indian kid's body inside and examined it. We sent a recovery team in to evacuate the ER staff, who have all now died. The recovery team tried to collect the prospector, who was uncooperative and was terminated."

Even with what had happened before, Aniru and Isabella couldn't believe what they were hearing. Dr. Foege continued, "The Disciples continued on to Las Vegas, after they dropped the kid's body, to get to some kind of fucking soul-saving revival bullshit. The Disciples interacted with the people at the revival and died. Of course, all of the Disciples were *hot*, they had to be extremely hot, having been exposed to the dying Indian kid. But the people who came to the revival dispersed, to God knows where. We have reports of people collapsing at the airport, with 666 symptoms. We, Dr. Kitchen and Dr. Conteh, are at the beginning of an international nightmare... There is no antidote, and we can see no way of stopping this thing. I brought you here to see if in your experiences with the 666, there is any way, *any way* for Christ's sake, to stop it from killing countless millions?"

Aniru looked up at Dr. Foege and said, "Good God, who are you people? How can this planet even continue to exist with bastards like you running it."

Isabella added, "When we encountered the 666 both in the United States and in Africa, there was no way to stop it. Then when we learned how it had been spliced together and what the activation and deactivation triggers were... it's at this point inconceivable as to how to stop not only its continual spread, but we are, apparently, also seeing its mutation. The only way I can imagine halting it is through incineration. Which is inconceivable also. Unless there is something in its genetic code that would reveal a chromosomal vulnerability, then we are looking at a developing global disaster."

Dr. Foege bowed his head as if praying, "What have we done, God forgive me, what have we done...?" He didn't say another word as he walked out of the SCIF. When Aniru and Isabella exited the SCIF CDC security were running down the hallway and onto a waiting elevator. The head of security met them at the end of the corridor and ushered them into a conference room. "Dr's Kitchen and Conteh, there is a situation, Dr. Foege left your meeting, went to his office and shot himself. Can you tell me what your meeting concerned?"

Isabella and Aniru looked at each other, "No sir, I am sorry, but we cannot. If you want more information, contact the White House," Isabella said. Then they turned and left.

# Chapter 42

THE PRESIDENT WAS NOTIFIED of Dr. Foege's suicide. In but a few minutes he contacted Dr. Prokiv. "He's dead, he fucking killed himself..."

"Mr. President, what are you talking about?" Dr. Prokiv, hearing the panic desperation in the President's voice, asked.

"Foege blew his brains out, he had a meeting with Kitchen and Conteh, left the meeting and shot himself."

"So, Kitchen and Conteh have been briefed then?"

"How are you always so fucking cold, matter of fact, the fucking world's going to end... and *we* did it!" The President's voice was consumed with panic. Dr. Prokiv made no mention of Dr. Foege. "Mr. President, I would suggest that you immediately gather your staff, brief them within limits of need to know regarding the depth of the development of 666, then schedule a press conference explaining that a 'new viral entity has emerged, likely, from an environmental acquisition. Then add... it appears to have the ability to infect new hosts with an aggressive trajectory, that trajectory is beginning to emerge in newly discovered transmissions and unfortunately deaths. We are working day and night to discover what the nature of this virus is and how we can stop it. We are forming a task force to stop this new virus and to save as many Americans as possible. However, and I want to be honest with you, there are likely to be many deaths of our fellow citizens. I will keep you apprised of the task forces work as they progress. They will have the full cooperation and resources of the United States government at their disposal."

It sounded like Dr. Prokiv had already prepared this kind of hogwash in advance, just in case anything went awry. "Dr. Prokiv, how many deaths are we looking at, both in the United States and globally?"

"Mr. President, the plague killed between 75 and 200 million people, between 1346 and 1353, we could be looking at well exceeding those numbers, especially when we consider population density and the mechanism of international and relatively immediate travel."

"Dr. Prokiv, with Foege now dead..." the President said, "...no one outside of Kitchen and Conteh and the people at Dugway, by the way, I have ordered Dugway locked down... know anything about this. You are going to have to assume temporary responsibility of the CDC and we are going to have to get a new conference together. If we put the blame for this on a foreign country then we run the risk of demands from both parties for a massive response, given the nature of this thing, possibly even a nuclear response. So *how* we present this is critical... You, Dr. Prokiv, you write this, and I will deliver it to the American people... Likely in the next several hours..." At that point the President simply terminated the call.

He immediately contacted his wife to make sure she was at Cheyenne and the Mountain had been secured. Three hours later Dr. Prokiv arrived at the CDC and called for an emergency meeting with all the branch heads.

# Chapter 43

WHEN ISABELLA AND CONTEH left the CDC, there was no chopper waiting for them. Conteh said, "Things are going to move very quickly now, *it's* loose, there is no way to stop it. Two hundred fifty million years ago, 90% of the earth's population was wiped out, this could be what we are facing. And these bastards, these dirty bastards made it..." Isabella's voice a mix of *Christ what's coming* and rage. "It will erupt very soon..."

It was *happening*. People were beginning to show up at ERs. Each hour the numbers were doubling. Doctors didn't know what they were even trying to treat, but they did know, whatever it was, it was a killer. Massive volumes of calls were coming into the CDC. The Viral Special Pathogens Branch was alerted, but they had no idea what the source of such a viral entity could be. Airports, train stations, bus stations were seeing people expressing symptoms and dying. News stations were interrupting their regular programming and reporting that people, "Within the last several days, people are being reported to be dying from some kind of virus that is striking many of the larger western cities in the United States. It also appears that the same thing is beginning to show up now throughout the U.S. We are reaching out to the CDC, to try and learn what information they have, and as of yet, we have only been told that they have no information and are as confused about what appears to be an unknown disease entity. From our reporters in the field, emergency rooms are becoming overwhelmed with patients, and... these patients... Clearly, ladies and gentlemen, something very serious is occurring here... We will interrupt once we have further information."

**Chapter 44**

"Thank you all for coming, I am Dr. Theodore Prokiv and I have been working closely with the President of the United States on a matter of grave urgency that has developed. I have, at the request of the President, been asked to assume temporary command of the CDC, due to the tragedy of Dr. Foege's suicide and the nature of what we are now facing. This has escalated very quickly, and we have to be aware of what we are dealing with, that is one of the reasons I am here as well as working with you to develop a *coordinated* response.

"Let me brief you on what has occurred. Several years ago, at the Dugway Proving Ground, a group of virologists were tasked with developing a response, should there be a terrorist attack using biological weapons. Of course, this program was by nature top secret and only known to the scientists at Dugway, the President and myself. The program developed a tripart viral entity that was intended to counteract a biological weapons attack. As you know, the Biological and Toxin Weapons Convention was signed in 1972. But, of course, like all nations, the United States continues with developing counter measures and vaccines for potential threats. The work as Dugway has been the cornerstone for our potential counter measure response. A tripart viral entity, combining Zaire Ebola, Marburg and the measles virus, was developed using a special gene-splicing technique, developed at Dugway. The virus in tests proved to be a highly contagious and virulent. But there was a caveat to it, which is important as we move forward. It could only be activated by a unique UHF signal and deactivated with a unique EHF signal. But, once it is activated and the virus reaches a bioactive level in the human body and begins to replicate, then the *countdown* begins as to how long we have to use the

EHF signal to deactivate the virus. If someone is exposed to the virus, it would be completely inert until it was activated by the UHF signal. It would produce no symptoms and it would be undetectable by blood or tissue sampling. It appears that the virus was <0nm in size. Yes, I know this is not possible, but regardless... This by definition was developed as a counter measure only, obviously the United States would *never* use such a counter measure device offensively. We do not know how but the tripart viral entity escaped from the Dugway laboratory and in an unexplainable development, it appears that the unique UHF code to viral activation has been compromised. Plus, it also appears the virus mutated, which has shortened its bioactivation timeline and begins systematic destruction shortly after it is activated. Once this occurs it becomes the most infectious viral agent ever known to man. At this point, we have no way to stop its progression. We are using a *concentric circle epidemiology configuration* to understand the highest to lowest levels of exposure lethality. This is similar to understanding the concentric circle lethality of nuclear weapon impacts of the early 1950s, during the cold war. The primary kill zone will obviously be at the center of the circle; these are the large population zones and then we reduce the number of deaths as we move out to the farthest point of the circle. Millions of people are going to succumb to this virus. The President will be giving a press conference later today and the little about what we know will be made public. This was clearly a tragic mistake. What I would like for you to do, specifically in the VSPB, is to look for points of disruption with the virus. We can work with the virus as an entity robotically, but not directly in a BSL-4 lab, as there may be an issue of full protection with PPEs. I can take a few questions but there are aspects to the virus and its development that I won't discuss, also to reiterate, the President will be delivering a different message. Let me be clear, ladies and gentlemen: Should *anything, anything* that was discussed in this room today be leaked by any individual, in anyway, *each* and *every* person assembled today, as well as their family, will be taken into immediate custody. Therefore, you will all keep your mouths shut."

# Chapter 45

"THE ONLY POSSIBILITY, AS I see it," Isabella said, "is that we find out who the Popobawa is. We know that he apparently, as fate would have it, intersected with the Indian boy at the Peach Springs Trading Post. Activates the virus and then goes on his way. But again, the question remains, who is this man?"

Aniru responded: "So, we have to see if we can somehow figure out who he is and what he has made that he is using to activate the virus. But the transmission of the virus is going to be exponential, and millions of people are going to die before anything, *anything* at all can be done."

Aniru then said, "If Prokiv will release the EHF code for deactivation, then perhaps the virus can be deactivated before it reaches a critical mass. If he makes a declaration of national security, and will not, then the only alternative is to find the Popobawa and to find out how he stumbled onto the proper code sequences."

Isabella followed, "Prokiv is a cold, calculating sadistic bastard, look what he did in Africa to Chidinma's village and to the Indian Reservation, I don't see him releasing those codes. Plus he is the only one who would have access to the complete code parameters, because in these kind of top secret operations, the scientists have all their research compartmentalized, very few people have access to *all* of the information about a project, specific aspects of the these operations are holed away, then those who do have clearance to the entirety of the project bring those parts together, and from what I saw in the meeting at Camp David we were ordered to, Prokiv is the *only* one who knows everything."

"It is difficult to believe that someone, who has the ability to at least mitigate the number of lives, would refuse to do so, that is savage!" Aniru said.

Isabella looked at Aniru, "Do you know about the *whole-body radiation* studies done in Cincinnati by Dr. Eugene Saenger?" Aniru said he had no idea who Saenger was. Isabella continued, "Saenger's work was in every way disputable, sadistic, reprehensible, my parents actually had some dealings with him very early on in Paintsville. He contacted my father, wanting him to send miners with advanced lung cancer to the University of Cincinnati Hospital so he could do whole body radiation on them. When my father asked him about the amount of irradiation they would be given, Saenger said it was, '300 rad of Cobalt-60 in an hour.'"

Aniru, not prone to loud outbursts, said, "What the hell, that's equal to twenty-thousand chest x-rays!"

"So later then," Isabella told Aniru, "...Saenger continued for years at the University of Cincinnati hospital and Cincinnati Children's Hospital, tagging patients with advanced cancers, got grants from the Defense Department Support Agency and between somewhere around 1958 and 1971 he exposed *hundreds* of poor, hell most of the patients didn't even speak English, Blacks and Hispanics to these massive radiation doses. He and another physician named Edward Silberstein considered *those* people write offs. And of course, they *all* died horrid, painful deaths from massive radiation poisoning. They were all cremated and buried in lead-lined urns.

"The reason was... the Defense Department wanted to know how long a soldier could live, if he was exposed to the radiation effects of a nuclear explosion on the battlefield, how far beyond the initial kill zone, could he keep functioning, keep shooting, killing the enemy, how fucking long before he collapsed and died from the radiation exposure. So... this isn't the first time the government has considered human beings as expendable chattel. By the way, my father told him to go to hell. My mother said he should be dipped in honey and strapped to a tree in the Smokey Mountains... let the bears have their way with him. There is no way to avert this, it has begun, the only possibility is to mitigate the number of deaths."

Aniru stated the obvious: "Airports, train and bus stations are already seeing people dropping and dying."

Isabella said, "I think, even though I am sure the army is trying to trace the Popobawa down, this is what we are exceptionally good at, let's go to the Peach Springs Trading Post, and try to trace his steps. The problem is we have is the risk of being infected."

Aniru nodded in agreement and said, "We, though, are the only ones on the planet who know what group of symptoms to look for, we know what the early symptoms are, we keep our distance and at the first sign of anyone expressing symptoms we leave as fast as we can. We have to contact Chidinma and have her meet us at the trading post, give her the directions, coordinate when we can all arrive, and we all should hire a private plane to get us there and not go by any public transportation."

Isabella agreed and followed with, "If we are going to die then at least let's die with a purpose."

Chidinma received the call about three in the afternoon, Isabella said she couldn't talk about the situation on the phone, but wanted Chidinma to make arrangements to meet she and Aniru at the Trading Post. Chidinma, of course, was hearing the reports and broadcasts about some kind of virus killing people and causing mass panic. When she talked to her mother, Chidinma knew Isabella wouldn't be telling her to meet them if it wasn't critical. It would be the next day before they all convened at the Peach Springs Trading Post. It wasn't long before Chidinma was briefed, and they began to lay out a plan to find the Popobawa.

The FBI had already been there asking questions and seeing if there was any CCTV. There was none. Isabella and Aniru asked the clerk who had been there the day the Popobawa had attacked the young Indian boy, if she could remember how the confrontation had occurred. "He kinda of waddled, you know what I mean, like a duck… The lady he was with was like one of the mean nuns I had at Indian school. The Indian boy, he was real sick, and the nun lady didn't like being bumped into, but the boy couldn't hold himself up, he wasn't trying to bother her, he just kinda fell into her, he'd just come out of the desert, I saw him out of the bathroom window when I was peeing, but she got real upset, you could see it on her face, the man she was with left the store and came back in with a small bag and held it out at the boy, and wow, did he start, you know, just kinda going crazy, jerking all over the place, howling, like two cats doing it out your window at night, you know what I mean? Then they paid for the things they had in their arms and just left.

"There was something though, huh, I forgot to tell those cops in suits that were here before, the man, when they were checking out said something about going to stop at Truxton, just up the road, there ain't nothing there, don't know if there's even a hundred folks there or not, they got the only motel around these parts, not much to look at, but Molly keeps the bed linin worshed and the rugs vacuumed, its Molly's place, see... Molly, shes a midget and it's only got eight rooms and it helps her get by, she's got a step ladder she stands on to check the guests in and out. Now there's *nothin* to do in Truxton, my boyfriend and I have stayed at Molly's, that's how I know the beds are clean, so if they did stay there, they're long gone by now."

Chidinma looked Truxton up on the map and said it was just down Route 66, it "won't take long for us to get there."

Fifteen minutes later they pulled up to Molly's. Chidinma looked up and saw the neon sign flashing *Molly's* on and off. Underneath in small letters it said, "*Molly's Inn, Dreary Guests, Easy and Tranquil.*" Beside the flashing sign was what appeared to be a life size image of Molly. When they went inside the small lobby, a woman who could only be Molly took two rungs up a step ladder and asked in a smoky voice how she could help them. Isabella began asking her about a couple a few days ago. "The man had a waddle and the woman looked like an embittered nun," Isabella said. "Yeah, what about them, they're still here, over there in number three." For a moment it was, as Aniru would later say, like the cliche, that time had stopped.

Molly took a key from a peg board and led Isabella, Aniru and Chidinma across the parking lot to room three. A few yards before they approached the door, Isabella and Aniru stopped and looked questionably at each other, Isabella reached out and took Chidinma's arm, holding her back. Molly stepped forward and began knocking on the door. Aniru said, "Mam, no one is going to answer, come back from the door..."

# Chapter 46

"Have all precautions been taken care of this time?"

"The timing is off and now we have a fucking mess, bodies are every goddamn where, hell we don't even know if *we* will make it out alive, Prokiv..."

"Mr. President, the only other fountainhead of the cessation codes has now been closed."

"So, as it stands, I am the *only* source for the complete code configuration, the other breach has been resolved."

"There is no other way of eliminating what could be the origins of how the activation and cessation codes were discovered without creating suspicion, so I believe it is best to let that part of any equation die on the vine."

"I sure as hell hope you are right, Prokiv..." The President responded.

"Sir," Dr. Prokiv said, "This is now set in motion and there is no way to stop its spread, without the cessation codes it *is* unstoppable. When the virus has done the job, and as you know, it is intended for you, Mr. President, to announce a breakthrough in its elimination and then initiate the cessation code protocol. You, Mr. President, will be credited with saving millions of lives, and... Mr. President, even with the best laid plans that go from A to Z, there is, somewhere between B through Y, where something gets fucked-up. The key is to discover the B through Y breach and close it before it can completely derail the rest of the planned operation, and again, Sir, we have done that. People like stories that they can perfectly follow, well in reality there are none of those."

The President spoke up, "Prokiv, I don't want you coming to the White House, anything that can't be discussed on a secure line I want

to take place at the bunker at Camp David."
"Understood, Mr. President."

# Chapter 47

ISABELLA TOLD MOLLY TO go back to the motel office, taking the key to room three from her. Aniru walked toward the window of the room and looked in as best he could. The closer he got to the room, the more the smell of death permeated. He and Isabella knew all too well the smell of human decomposition from their work in Africa. Rotting bodies being hauled to open pit graves, the pall of the putrescine stench rising from the corpses like a vaporous Satan coming up from Hell.

The curtains were open slightly enough at the bottom of the window that Aniru could see the body of a woman, slung backward across the bed, a single bullet hole in her skull, with a pool of blood puddled beneath her head. There were no obvious signs of the virus' torrent of destruction that Aniru could see through the window. Aniru told Isabella it looked safe to go in. Isabella unlocked the door, the sudden waft of putrefied air came rushing out of the room, Chidinma had certainly smelled death, but the abruptness of the odor made her wretch. The three of them went into the room. Robert was tied to a chair and shot in the same manner as Althea. He looked like he had been beaten before he was killed. Isabella figured Althea had been shot first, she not having any information to give whoever the killers were. The other thing that was clearly obvious was that their hands had been cut off. Whoever had done this didn't want Robert and Althea's identity discovered too quickly. Aniru looked at Robert and said, "And we have no idea who he is... There is nothing in here either, everything is gone."

Isabella said, "Let's look at their bodies."

Chidinma and Aniru lifted Althea until she was fully on the bed.

They undressed her carefully and examined her body. There was nothing telling. Isabella had learned back in Kentucky to never go anywhere without a pocketknife, which she had taken out and cut away the bindings on Robert. Aniru and Chidinma helped lower Robert to the floor and then undress him. As they looked over his body, nothing on initial examination looked telling. But as they rolled him from back to front, Isabella proclaimed, "My God, look at this..."

Aniru spoke up and said, "Yes, it's an old smallpox scar on his arm."

Isabella said, "Yes, *but* my God I have never seen one of these, I have read about them but never seen one."

Aniru and Chidinma looked puzzled. "Look..." Isabella pointed to the indented scar. "Look around the permitter of the scar, do you see the star like edging?" Aniru acknowledged he did while Chidinma nodded. "This is a scar from *dermatofibrosarcoma protuberans*. The tumor itself is a rare sarcoma but... with that edging, this is a *very* rare side effect to the smallpox vaccine. There have only been three or four cases in history. We can figure out who he is that way. Plus, there isn't a chance in hell that whoever killed them would be able to figure that out!"

Aniru said, "They will have no way of knowing we have the means to track down his identity."

Chidinma said, "We should get out of here... the Popobawa is dead."

They made sure everything was put back as it was, with the exception of Althea and Robert's bodies and then left. Isabella went to the office before they pulled away and told Molly to call the sheriff and not to go inside the room. Both parties were deceased.

# Chapter 48

IN BUT A FEW short weeks the world had turned over. Like a lake turning over, the top mixing with the bottom and the bottom with the top. The death toll from the 666 was devastating.

There were few places that had escaped the virulence of the virus. Extremely isolated villages here and there or islands with small populations and almost impossible to get to.

The President had retreated to Cheyenne Mountain with his family and cabinet. He was running the country from there. Dr. Prokiv had commandeered the bunker at Camp David. The CDC was still in operation, but many of its staff had succumbed also. When the virus had hit the airports and train stations, all hopes of containment were lost. It wasn't long after that the President had ordered all mass transit sites closed. By then it was too late.

Even though it was a manufactured virus, and its release was born of arrogant incompetence, there was little preparation for this kind of event at the CDC and other governmental agencies regardless. A constant bureaucratic nightmare had the scientists feeling like they were constantly walking in cold molasses. Now with at least half of the earth's population at risk, there were no answers on the horizon. The usual isolation orders were in place, there was limited means of mass transportation and those not infected were for the most part doing whatever they thought was necessary to stay that way. People had shot their neighbors, retreated to the woods where highly forested areas had become tent city enclaves, signs telling encroachers that they would be shot, *no* exceptions, if they crossed a line of demarcation, "*Including women and children!*" There was no attempt at treating anyone who showed up at hospitals, as there was none. Mass graves were dug in every major city, as funeral parlors had shuttered their doors, how could they not. Bodies were scooped up and hauled away to the closest grave site, covered in lye, burned, and then covered over. It was like the plague years of Europe had returned to this century. The *civilized* offended by the sight and stench of the dead. But, there were no castle walls.

Periodically the President would deliver a message that all was being done that could be done and government scientists were working "furiously..." to figure a way to contain the situation. In a late afternoon meeting, the President called Dr. Prokiv, "What are you going to do about this, Prokiv?"

"Mr. President, as you are well aware, this project was designed to bring the population to a manageable level. We have almost reached our goal, this *had* to be done, sir, there was no way left to curtail how out of control things had gotten. There were no limits any longer, things were becoming uncivilized. Sir, you know we had countless discussions on this, looked at bringing some kind of sanity..."

"Dr. Prokiv, this has to be brought under control soon, this wasn't set to go forward until much later and then this Indian kid fucked everything up and now we have shit on our hands..."

"Yes, Mr. President, that is true, but once we decide when to at least begin to use the satellite system to broadcast the EHF code to deactivate the virus then those infected with the virus and who have not reached the threshold point will stop being a vector. Those who have crossed the threshold of infectivity will, with current precautions, simply die off. You, sir, will of course announce in an emergency broadcast the discovery that will thwart the advance of the virus, and Mr. President, due to the circumstances that currently necessitates the cessation any change in the current administration, until order can be restored, and the threat is quelled. Mr. President, you have the opportunity to become the greatest president in the history of the United States and a worldwide savour. I envy you. Sir, human beings are gullible, and they want more than anything to find a victor, one who they can imagine is lionhearted... This, Mr. President, is *your* lionhearted moment...

"Realize, sir, that no one, *no one* would believe that this set of circumstances could happen, that anyone could conceive of this kind of stratagem, much less put it into action, well, sir, we are just about to bring it to complete fruition."

"All right, Prokiv... but this has to end soon. Cheyenne Mountain is getting old... It is on complete lockdown and the presidential advance team and alert task force have taken command here. Our quarters are secured from the rest of the mountain, and once it is time to make the announcement to the American people, we will make it from here. The broadcast center of course is a facade of the south wall of the Oval Office, so no one will know I am temporarily located here."

# Chapter 49

"HELLO, DR. WALTON, THIS is Isabella Kitchen, I certainly imagine you have your hands full with what has happened..."

"It is good to hear from you, Dr. Kitchen, yes and of course, I mean my God the number of deaths, everyone is terrified, and there isn't a damn thing to fight it with. We did try an experimental single-antigen measles vaccine we developed here, just to try to slow the infectability of the virus, not that it would have any effect on the other two virus' themselves, but we wanted to see if we could reduce the number of people becoming infected so fast. Unfortunately, we believe the virus has mutated well beyond that. Anyway, what can I do for you Dr. Kitchen?"

"Dr. Walton, I am sorry about what is happening, it is ghastly, this thing is a nightmare virus. But obviously you developed the protocol for managing large scale pandemics, there couldn't be anyone better to handle this on a day-to-day basis.

"I was wondering, Dr. Walton, I am doing some background research on a very rare reaction to the smallpox vaccine, *dermatofibrosarcoma protuberans, DFSP.* I need to know the dates these cases were reported on, the physicians who wrote the case up and where they were located. It's for a course I am developing on triangulation and epidemiology, I believe there have only been four cases since the 1940s."

"Dr. Kitchen, I'd be pleased to pull that information, it will give me a break, even if just for a few minutes from the 666... I remember Dr. Kitchen, you are the one who, now way back called this damn virus the 666, before anybody knew anything about it!"

"Yes, Dr. Walton, that was indeed me."

"Thank you for getting the other information on DFSP for me, do you have a timeline, given your schedule?"

"I will have it tomorrow morning."

## Chapter 50

TED PROKIV, PH.D., HAD been a brilliant student when he was at Stanford. He got his Ph.D. at nineteen in biophysical chemistry. His dissertation, *Reimagining Biological Warfare: The Mighty Microbe Goes Too War,* began to set him on the path of not only reimagining biological warfare, but also reimagining the world order. "We are moving beyond our means to take care of ourselves as a species..." he would tell his students in the seminars he taught at the National War College. "This cannot be sustained, the population is increasing at an exponential level, and... this is critical to understand, the educational level is not even coming close to keeping a parallel pace. As the worldwide population grows, we see an inverse relationship with a realistic conceptualization of how the actual number of human beings can physically occupy the planet. It isn't just about population density though, it is also about needing to *cleanse,* if you will, the population of what we might refer to as overgrowth and then to create a system that will monitor what is left, after the overgrowth is culled, and then to develop a system of government that will, as one of its primary responsibilities to its governing population, maintain a dedicated, well managed order." Many of the students at the NWC were sympathetic with Dr. Prokiv. Understanding his words as a reflection on the concept of war itself. During one of the seminars, a students interrupted Dr. Prokiv, saying, "What you are saying, sir, is much like bringing the concept of war from a state of chaos and disarray to a state of ongoing management. So that war, as we have come to know it, is no longer a threat that hangs over our heads, or something that one nation threatens another with, but that which, in essence, brings about a *smoothing* of society. So, there isn't such a state of constant chaos, but the establishment of a world order that would remain less blemished. Less *warty*..." Dr, Prokiv, as those comments were more and more in line with his position, nodded in agreement.

He moved quickly from the NWC to a position of advising senators and congressmen, and then being queried by those with presidential aspirations. It wasn't long before the harmony of a mutual mindset was in place.

# Chapter 51

Dr. Walton phoned Isabella the following morning. "Dr. Kitchen. Yes, there have been four cases since the 1940s. One of the individuals who developed DFSP was a child, seven years old. It looks like, in looking back over the write up, that the smallpox vaccine decimated her immune system. The child developed DFSP about nine months after the inoculation, but she was reportedly very sickly up until she developed DFSP and then succumbed to it, far sooner than anyone would have thought. The other two, well both authors of the papers have died long ago and the fourth, Elizabeth E. Tibbo, M.D., Ph.D. is currently at Penn State Medical School. She had the fourth case back in the early seventies. A nine-year-old boy, smallpox vax and then six months later he developed DFPS."

"Thank you, Dr. Walton." Isabella turned to Aniru and Chidinma and said, "We are going to Hershey, Pennsylvania." The drive from Atlanta to Hershey took about ten hours. There was little traffic on I-85. Isabella had contacted the medical school and found that Dr. Tibbo was retired from both practice and teaching, except for the occasional seminar. The medical school was gracious enough to contact Dr. Tibbo and arrange for Isabella, Aniru and Chidinma to meet her at her home.

The three of them were greeted by a long-time gray haired, distinguished woman, now with arthritic knees not doing all too well from carrying too much weight. "I am pleased to meet you. Your reputations obviously proceed you. And... Dr. Chidinma Kitchen, I hope your work carries on your family tradition of excellence."

Isabella moved straight to the reason of their visit. "Dr. Tibbo, Dr. Walton from the CDC was able to get me your name as the researcher who had published the last paper on the post smallpox vaccine related DFSP. The reason I wanted your name is because we believe that individual may hold the key to resolving the epidemic."

"Good Christ..." Dr. Tibbo said.

"The virus is activated and thus deactivated by some UHF/EHF signal frequency. The government, well, we are not sure, but we believe has those frequencies. But... they are highly classified, and why they are not being used to stop or at least mitigate how it is being transmitted, we are not sure. But we believe the individual in your post smallpox inoculation DFSP case may be an individual who inadvertently stumbled onto the codes and activated the virus, an accidental Typhoid Mary. We recently examined the body of a man who appeared to be in his late forties and who had left deltoid scarring, consistent with a post vax DFSP surgical site. So, this individual is dead then..." Dr. Tibbo said. "Yes... he was murdered, along with his female companion."

"Doctors, let me check my old records. I have kept all of my old files, I have never been one to destroy medical or research records, so much information is there... everything I have will eventually go to the UPenn medical archives. Please come with me."

Aniru, Isabella and Chidinma walked behind Dr. Tibbo, out behind her house to a barn-like structure. It had a lock through a loop hasp, which she unlocked. Inside were dozens of file cabinets, all labeled with dates and in terms of her research, nomenclature to indicate the condition she was investigating at the time. Dr. Tibbo, without hesitation, went to a file cabinet, opened a drawer, leafed through the countless folders, until she came upon one that said, 'S-pox: Dermatofibrosarcoma protuberans.'

Opening the folder, Dr. Tibbo scanned the page with her index finger. "The young man's name was Robert Shufflebottom, odd name, I remember thinking. But that was his name. He was from Philly. Here is the address, at the time, I can't imagine anyone from the family is still there, but... But certainly, with a name like that, there can't be too many of them in the phone book."

The original address Dr. Tibbo gave them was now boarded up row houses. The only Robert Shufflebottom in the Philadelphia phone book now lived on Roosevelt Blvd., in the Oxford Circle neighborhood, in the lower Northeast section of Philadelphia. When

Isabella, Aniru and Chidinma pulled up in front of the house, they saw a well-tended lawn, purple daffodils standing tall and a freshly paved driveway.

As they walked around the house, looking into each window, everything looked in perfect order. Absolutely *perfect*. Everything they could see looked like it had been arranged, not only aesthetically but also geometrically. Knick-knacks were arranged on a long cadenza witting against a wall seemingly all at 45-degree angles, pictures also were hung as though the hanger had been more concerned with their size and proportion than if the art was pleasing or provocative. Also, there was no theme to the art, everything just seemed random. The house looked like the person who lived there asked someone to come in and decorate it for them.

There was one room toward the back of the house, and off the kitchen, that was obviously Robert's. Through the window they could see a large drafting table with what looked like an electronics schematic laying on top of it. There was also a slide-rule that had clearly been used as the slide was not flush with the sides. Oddly, hanging above the drafting table, was a gun of some sort. Isabella said, "Look hanging on the wall, is that a gun?" Aniru, looking over Isabella's shoulder, "It looks like a toy, sometimes in the village the missionaries would come and bring old black and white science fiction movies. They would be sure and say that no matter how far you blasted into space, you could never blast your way into Heaven. That could only happen by accepting Jesus as your savior. I asked one of the missionaries where Heaven was. He said, no one can know the directions to Heaven unless you dedicate your life to spreading Jesus' love... Then I said, if I accept Jesus as my savior, like you say, then do I get a map? The missionary, I remember, was white and fat, then he slapped me across the face, turned and walked away. I could hear him mumbling that he'd find another soul that was worthy of Jesus' love. But, in the movies the pilot of the rocket always had a ray gun that looked just like that!" Isabella and Chidinma stared into the window aghast at what they were seeing. "Jesus," Isabella said, "Could *that* be what the hell has caused this nightmare?" To which Chidinma said, "Who the hell was this guy?"

Aniru and Chidinma waited while Isabella walked across the lawn to one of the neighbors. When she knocked at the door a woman, about eighty, answered. "Hello, I am Dr. Kitchen, and we are trying to find the gentleman who lives next door, Mr. Shufflebottom, I believe, can you by any chance tell me where he works"? The woman seemed to have just awoken. But she looked at Isabella and said, "I haven't seen Bobby in a month of Sunday's. How is he?"

"Well, we just need to talk to him, and we aren't sure where he works, if you know it would be a big help."

"Oh sweetheart, he works at Calderon... he's an electrical engineer, Bobby designed that toy gun a few years ago that everyone was talking about. Did you know that the government tried to have it taken off the market, but once that happened, well oh dear, all the little boys wanted one and the girls too. Bobby was so proud of himself, he's a very likeable man, he comes over about once a week or so and sees if I need anything." Snarling, the lady then said, "Well he did, until he got mixed up with that *woman*. Every time he came over after she wormed her way into his life, well that's what I think, she'd be right behind him after a few minutes or so, and right when Bobby said 'do you need anything?' she'd always say, dear you don't have time for that, remember we are going some damn place, oh gosh, pardon my mouth, she just irks me..." Isabella thanked her, wanting to find out where Calderon Toy Company was.

# Chapter 52

Dr. Prokiv was well entrenched at Camp David. Much of the government's day to day operations of nonessential services had temporarily shuttered until the crisis was over. He made regular calls to the senior management staff at the CDC, knowing full well they had no answers, and he could care less. The nitwit who had stumbled on the activation and deactivation codes had been eliminated as a variable. How he had discovered the codes and how he had come in contact with those infected was now, *especially* now, of no concern to Dr. Prokiv. Things had progressed too far. If the President could maintain his demeanor and do what he was told, then time would dictate how long the global pandemic would continue. He didn't think of himself as a wicked man. But rather, he saw himself as a savior of sorts. If things weren't thinned out then it wouldn't matter. Few would hold him in high regard if they knew how this had all been put in place. But he had no need for aggrandizement either while he was of this earth or after he wasn't. From the first moment he had met the President, he knew he was a mealy man. There was nothing to him, hollow. Dr. Prokiv once told a whore, whom he saw regularly, that he thought of the President as a man you could drop a marble in his mouth and two seconds later it would fall out his ass. There was nothing inside of him, no scaffolding and certainly no guts. He thought what he was doing was courageous. The only courage the President had ever known was eating something without one of his lacky's tasting it first. His wife, the first lady, well she may have been the first but she sure as hell wasn't a lady. As far as Dr. Prokiv was concerned, she rode a fucking broom. When Prokiv was done with them, they would be easy enough to rid himself of.

# Chapter 53

THE CALDERON TOY COMPANY was on Washington Avenue. It set in between a long-shuttered textile manufacturer and an import/export company. The floorboards were clearly from the turn of the century and probably still had dirt and dust dating back a hundred years, buried in the crevasses of where they joined together.

Isabella, Aniru and Chidinma walked into the front entrance and asked to see the president of the company, saying it was a matter of national importance. Isabella still had her CDC identification. Shortly after they had made their way through the morass of toys being assembled by workers who, Aniru would say later, looked like they wished they were dead, they were met by an old woman who creaked as much as the floors, whose index and middle fingers had indentations from years crimping a cigarette and who walked with a decisive limp. Clearly, she was there when the first board had been nailed down. "Hello, I am Ethyl, Mr. Piedmont is tied up right now, how can I help you; I am his assistant?" Isabella showed Ethyl her ID and said she needed to interrupt him; it was a matter of immediate importance.

In a few minutes Ethyl escorted the three of them into Mr. Piedmont's office. Isabella thought they had walked back in time. The windows looking out into the plant were full of bubbles that had cooled unevenly, making it look wavy. Each time a worker walked by, they looked like they were part of a silent movie and surrounded by toys from another era. "Hello Mr. Piedmont..." Isabella said, then introducing Aniru and Chidinma. "We understand a Mr. Robert Shufflebottom worked here?" Mr. Piedmont confirmed by nodding. "He still does, he is on an extended holiday." Aniru then said that

Robert was dead. He and his female companion had been murdered. They were at the toy company to get information on how he had developed what must have been the UHF and EHF frequencies.

Mr. Piedmont, having heard Robert was dead, dropped his head and said he had been with the company for many years and told them when Robert started out, "...he was called Little Bobby Two Shoes, I bet when he died his shoes didn't match. For some reason or other, Robert just never was able to match his shoes. I don't know how that worked out in the morning when he got dressed for work, but when he walked through the factory to his office, he shuffled, like his name, strange isn't it, more than walked and it brought attention to his mismatched shoes. The factory workers made up a song about him and hummed it when he went by. He never said much, he just went into his office and got to work. He came to me one day with a prototype of a toy ray gun. I couldn't believe it when he aimed it at me, my God, I just started itching all over, he said the kids would love it. I told him, he would have to tone down the effect it had when kids shot each other with it, he said he would just 'dial it back' so it didn't cause the kids to itch so much, and he did. Within weeks after we launched it, he called it the Garin Death Ray Pistol, or the GDRP. Good God, the kids loved it. We couldn't keep the stores supplied, they were selling out even before a new shipment arrived, then some damn committee, The Study Group for Raising Healthy Children, decided it should be taken off the market, they said it was a danger to the healthy development of children, that's when the demand went through the roof! Anyway, it has been our best seller, worldwide now for many years. But, what are you wanting, I don't understand what this has to do with this scourge?"

"Mr. Piedmont, we cannot get into specifics, but... we need the frequencies of what you call the GDRP... and I think we need access to Robert's working notes on how he went about developing this..."

"Well, of course you understand that is proprietary..." Piedmont said.

"Sir, this could bring about an end to the scourge, Robert appears to have stumbled upon a way of activating and deactivating this virus, I understand the proprietary nature of the codes but... this far outweighs those concerns..."

Chidinma then spoke up and said, "Mr. Piedmont, think about how Calderon Toy Company will be viewed as part of the solution to ending the death and suffering of millions of people, worldwide, your company will be talked about hundreds of years from now."

Mr. Piedmont called Ethyl and told her to open Robert's office and to give them access to anything they wanted.

In Robert's office was a tall oak bookshelf that winged into the corner. There, going from top to bottom, were dozens of artist sketch books, numbered with masking tape, 1-24 and dated, going back twenty years. Aniru, Isabella and Chidinma began pulling the books from the shelves, starting with number one, and working their way forward. The workbooks were filled with drawings and musings about Robert's ideas of making the most *perfect* toy ray gun. "Jesus, this guy was obsessed with this idea," Aniru said, as he thumbed through the first volume. Chidinma, in looking through Volume 15, discovered hundreds of engineering equations, drawings of radio towers and sketches of ray guns that were used in the silent movies. Robert had even drawn a sketch of a small, deformed man, almost hunchback aiming his ray gun at a sinister looking monster. On the next page, the buckled hunchback was standing with one foot on the chest of the defeated heathen.

As Isabella began to examine one of the later workbooks, she began to see a trend. Robert's equations were now entirely focused on UHF/EHF wave structure. Not only was he looking at megahertz and gigahertz, but he was also examining how to alter the wave structure itself—Robert had written down the *wave equation*, "$\partial^2 u/\partial t^2 = c^2 \nabla^2 u$." Directly after the equation Robert had written, "...Alter the dimensionality and Modify the wave speed..." It was then that Isabella began to see what Robert had stumbled onto. He had not just, in essence, created a wave structure that inadvertently activated the virus, per se, but Robert also created a biological portal for *the*, then it hit her, *any* viral entity, either to become active or, as she conceptualized it, for the membrane of a potential biological ingress to become even more permeable, permitting a viral entity to go from a latent state, or deactivated state to an rapidly activated state.

"Christ..." Isabella said out loud, as she handed the workbook to Aniru and Chidinma. When Isabella took Aniru and Chidinma through her analysis, they were in awe of Robert's genius. Aniru looked at Isabella and said, "My God, if this man had been in medicine instead of *toys*... Jesus..."

"But," Chidinma spoke up and said, "if a scientist at Dugway developed this, why in the hell won't they use it to stop these deaths? This is a fucking worldwide calamity, I don't understand!"

## Chapter 54

It was shortly after the viral scourge began that Dr. May Ying of the Dugway Viral Development Group was in the BSL-4 lab examining a culture of Machupo virus, which caused the recent outbreak of Bolivian hemorrhagic fever in Magdalena. In the outer conference room, the other three members of the group were reviewing the status of their current projects.

Dr. Ying had just began notating that "...the particles released from this particular group of infected cells are characteristically pleomorphic and range in diameter from 50 to over 300 nano, augh..." It was then that Dr. Ying immediately became tachycardic and in those few seconds lost control of her bladder and bowels, she also began spewing white foam into her face mask. The hydrogen cyanide coming through her air supply was second by second binding to cytochrome oxidase, one of the enzymes in her respiratory chain, preventing the cells from using oxygen. In but a few seconds more, Dr. Ying began convulsing and going into full respiratory arrest. In another minute she was dead.

An exposure alarm went off throughout the facility when Dr. Ying's O2 had become disrupted when she fell to the floor convulsing. This caused an immediate lockdown of this section of the facility. Through the 15mm thick windows of the lab, the other scientists saw Dr. Ying laying on the floor of the BSL-4. They donned their exposure suits and made their way into the lab. Each scientist reached for an O2 line. And each scientist, one by one immediately suffered the same fate as Dr. Ying.

The official record said it was the result of a horrific accident. Somehow a hydrogen cyanide gas cylinder had been mislabeled and introduced into the air supply resulting in the death of the four scientists. The facility had centralized O2. So, a full investigation of how such an accident could occur would be conducted and further safeguards would be put in place, so it never happened again. A letter from the President to the scientist's family acknowledged and thanked them for their courageous work, which of course, due to the nature of which could not be discussed.

# Chapter 55

Dr. Prokiv had always considered himself a practical man. There was little in life he hadn't seen or done and now he wanted to weed the garden. As he had explained to his students and to the President, who whole heartedly agreed, but unlike Prokiv, his conviction was mere lip service. When Dr. Prokiv had proposed the idea of population thinning, the President had listened attentively, but it wasn't until Prokiv had convinced him that his hands would not be soiled if he too agreed to the necessity of pruning the vines. "With this, Mr. President, we will eliminate the undergrowth and the forest will flourish..."

The staff at Camp David only knew that Dr. Prokiv was to receive presidential level protection. And *that* he received. He was guarded around the clock and his work with the CDC on helping to find a solution to the scourge was done via phone calls. Hell, it didn't matter it was just for show anyway. No one had the key to scourges resolution except him. It would end when *he* said it would end. The thinning had to be a proper one. One that would hone out the riffraff, those who provide nothing and take the most, those engaging in despicable things that aren't even talked about other than between themselves. There was no other way. When the trash was swept from the house they could live in cleanliness. He would have said, *once again*, but in truth, it was a time that he nor anyone had ever known. Now, though, through his meticulous planning and implementation it was being brought about and almost complete.

Roughly one-third of the population of the earth had now perished. There needed to be another seventeen percent, and he would have accomplished what he set out to do. "Jesus," he thought to himself... "seventeen percent..." proud of his preciseness. As he had said many times, both to himself and the president, *one man*, yes *one*, if he knew what he was doing and then to keep a short tether on those in assist and… at the right moment, cut the tether and let those who had cleaved to, fall into the abyss, then, finally, *finally* one could breathe the deep, unencumbered breaths of complete emancipation. Dr. Prokiv's lungs were expanding more and more, hour by hour.

## Chapter 56

ISABELLA, ANIRU AND CHIDINMA now knew that the key, in addition to the frequencies, was the modification of the wave structure itself. The RNA of the virus must respond to the wave modification in a way that breaks it apart. It doesn't act on the body's immune system per se, instead it breaks apart the virus with the EHF signaling and furthers the cohesion of the tripart components of the virus with the UHF signal.

For countless years there has been the debate, are viruses even alive, are they living entities. Clearly the scientists at Dugway didn't immerse themselves in this controversy, they knew what *they* were doing but *equally* Robert did not "So," Isabella said, "...Robert, we should still call him the Popobawa, didn't have to answer the living virus question, he was only interested in causing a reaction to something he didn't know anything about."

"And then..." Aniru picked up, "if he wasn't bothered with the question, he could approach the reaction in strictly a mechanistic manner. But the folks at Dugway went around the virus question to the other side and they formerly didn't look at how to kill the virus with say an antiviral, they, I guess Dr. Amaechi, looked at breaking it apart."

To which, Chidinma said, "My God, like some opera singers can break glass with the frequency of their voice..."

"Okay," Aniru added, "We've got this, we have the equation and the wave modifications, so now how in the hell do we institute an intervention, we can't even call this a cure, per se. It will be a matter of deactivating the virus and saving those people whose membrane of a potential biological ingress hasn't fully opened to allow a lethal level of the virus to enter the host's body."

Isabella spoke up and said, "So this will be like the first class on viruses in med school. The virus, students, travels along the surfaces of X cells until its proteins begin to bind with receptors on those particular cells. Then the virus and the cells fuse, *viral copulation*, allowing the DNA or RNA inside the virus to enter the cells, where it begins to reproduce. If enough viral matter is able to penetrate host cells without being deactivated or delimited by a host's immune system, or other antiviral mechanism, infection begins in earnest."

"And in this case," Chidinma said, "You're dead..."

# Chapter 57

Isabella placed a call to the secure number that they had been given at the meeting with the President and Dr. Prokiv. As they were told the number was monitored 24 hours a day and it would immediately access the President's private alert system.

In less than ten minutes, Isabella, Aniru and Chidinma were on a conference call with the President. "Mr. President, we have the UHF/EHF frequencies for the virus activation and deactivation in our possession," Isabella said. The President was *stunned*. Dr. Prokiv had assured him that any possibility of acquiring these frequencies was virtually impossible. "My God, Dr. Kitchen, how, how were, where did you uncover these?" the President responded. "Sir, this is very convoluted, however, I believe we have worked out a planned response to the viral outbreak, one that, if you will grant us priority access, we believe we can implement in a *relatively* short period of time."

"Of course, this will not *cure* anyone, but... we believe it will deactivate the people who have *just* been infected," Aniru interjected.

Isabella then added, "This is very complicated from a virology standpoint, and suffice to say, this side of the discovery of the frequencies was reverse engineering the process of the man who stumbled upon them."

"It would be better if we could initiate our plan to bring the spread of this to a halt. As I said, we are not looking at a cure, that is not possible. But we can stop the spread by abating the viral virulence, by nullifying the impact on individuals whose exposure has been immediate. If we can then shut down, if you will, the virus's ability to gain a biological foothold, then we will begin the process of bringing this plague under control."

"Mr. President," Aniru said, "Dr. Kitchen and I have more

investigative and on the ground experience of any virologists in the world, no one has seen the spectrum of what we have been exposed to, and we are telling you our plan will work."

Isabella added, "This, sir, will take time, but we cut the viruses head off and we continue to isolate those who have become terminally ill beyond any possibility of recovery."

Chidinma spoke up and said, "Mr. President, imagine it is like a cat who has a clump of matted hair. You have to first cut as much of the clump of the mat out and then use a fine comb to free up the thicker and more bound mat nearer the cat's skin. This is exactly the same process, except obviously, on a considerably more macroscale."

"What is your recommendation?" the President asked.

"Mr. President, we are requesting full priority access to USAMRIID and ultimately the Army Corp of Engineers. This will take a military intervention globally, and only the full arms of the U.S. military have that capability. They can do the coordination and we can work with the scientists in terms of modifying current radar equipment, both military and civilian to recode their frequencies, we also have a plan as to how to use these systems with the general population."

The President could now see the wisdom of their logic, specifically from a re-election standpoint. It was also apparent to the President that fucking Prokiv no longer held all the cards.

"Doctors, under the Constitution of the United States, Article II, Section 2, Clause 1, The Commander in Chief Clause, grants the President just about any power to intervene, in any way to secure and protect the United States. I am now invoking this clause and sending an order as we speak, directly to the Commander at US-AMRIID and to the Joint Chiefs to grant you *full, immediate* and *unquestioning* access and authority to begin the resolution of this horrible outbreak that has killed so many countless millions. Please give me your location and I will have a chopper dispatched to gather you and take you directly to USAMRIID. The commander will meet you when you arrive, senior research staff will be assembled and ready to implement whatever you need for them to do. I assure you, you will not, under any circumstances, encounter any territorial issues." Isabella spoke up and said, "Sir, we appreciate your support, and we thank you." She then gave the President their location and awaited the arrival of the chopper.

"One more thing, Doctors, I will be making an emergency statement tonight to let the public know we are now beginning the road, albeit a long road, to recovery and the end to this tragedy. I will also be contacting my international counterparts and have them either feed my broadcast to their people or have them make a coordinated broadcast of my statement at the same respective time. Doctors, our country salutes you."

# Chapter 58

THE SUN WAS SIX degrees below the horizon, most people called it dusk, that Dr. Prokiv came up from the SCIF and stepped out onto the porch of the main cabin at Camp David. Two of his usual security detail had gone off duty, replaced by two agents whom he did not recognize.

As he stepped off the porch onto the asphalt of the circular drive, he noticed a dark van slowly bending with the curve. He then noticed that he had lost peripheral sight of the two men from his security detail, when he felt a cold metal object pressed against the back of his skull. In an imperceptible amount of time, three rounds from a suppressed .22 semi-automatic pistol entered Dr. Prokiv's skull and scrambled his brain. In whatever consciousness he had in those few milliseconds, he wondered how this could have occurred, and to *him*... then Dr. Prokiv left this earth and fell to the ground.

The two men opened the side door of the now awaiting van and climbed in. Prokiv's body was illuminated in a red glow from the taillights, as the van pulled away.

### Chapter 59

The MEDEVAC CHOPPER LANDED on one of the helipads at US-AMRIID. A staff car awaited Isabella, Aniru and Chidinma.

When Isabella had contacted Chidinma she had just completed her residency in internal medicine, with a specialty in infectious diseases, having a strong interest in developing effective long-term treatments of HIV. She was beginning the process of looking for places to hang her shingle when Isabella had called her and told her to drop everything, "You need to get to Arizona..." As Chidinma stepped out the chopper door, it all seemed illusory, *Jesus,* she thought, *I was born in a remote village in Liberia, my birth family all died, killed by a goddamn group of people who had written them off as even human, taken in and loved by the most amazing woman she had ever known and had a man in her life, from her own culture who loved her like his own blood, and... now this...*

They were taken to a SCIF. Assembled were the respective commanders of all representative departments and the Commander of USAMRIID and the Chairman of the Joint Chiefs. "Doctors, scientists and nonmedical personnel," Isabella said, "...we have been tasked by the President to institute what we believe is a solution of the scourge that has afflicted the world of almost half of its population. This is going to be a massive undertaking and one that ultimately will be met with resistance by some. We anticipate that there will be those who will refuse to participate in this process, and we respectfully demand that they be forced into compliance. This is not a voluntary action that we are recommending, it is mandatory. This plague is the result of what we believe to be an unconscionable plan that was instituted and not accidental. We further believe there is still more to discover with regard to how this came about. That, however, is not our task here.

"The viruses that have caused this outbreak is the result of a biological warfare program, regardless of the Biological and Toxic Weapons Convention of 1972. The virus is a tripart virus, combining two hemorrhagic fevers and the measles virus. As most of you know, the measles virus is a single-stranded, negative-sense RNA virus that belongs to the Paramyxoviridae family and the Morbillivirus genus, which makes it *highly* contagious. It was designed to be activated and deactivated by UHF and EHF frequencies, which were modifications of the actual wave structure of actual frequencies themselves. An individual who had absolutely *nothing* to do with the project accidentally stumbled upon the frequencies and their modification for use in, albeit it hard to imagine, a toy ray gun. We were able to locate his original work and believe current radar systems can be modified to generate the respective EHF frequencies to shatter the virus, or as my colleague, Dr. Chidinma Kitchen said, *like an opera singer shattering glass.*"

Aniru, then took the podium, "With the assistance of the Army Corp of Engineers, we want, the number is yet to be determined based on logistics, something akin to telescoping jetways. Modified into each jetway will be radar systems that will have been reengineered to generate the respective EHF frequency necessary to disrupt the actual structure of the 666 virus.

"Everyone in the population, regardless of obvious signs of infection, will be required to enter a jetway and be exposed to the EHF frequency. From what we have determined by witness reports of those who have been exposed to the activation of the virus by a specific UHF frequency, the wave was generated for approximately fifteen seconds. Therefore, we are recommending a thirty-second exposure time, fifteen seconds longer, simply as a cushion, of EHF to ensure proper deactivation, if the virus is present."

Then Chidinma also went to the podium: "We understand the monumental difficulty of this operation, but when someone is infected with the 666, they have to be reached *immediately*, for it is a death sentence. If we can just as immediately disrupt the actual *physical* structure of the virus, we believe we can cease its lethality. There needs to be a jetway in every ER in every hospital in the world, and logistically set up so that each segment of the population can receive the respective exposure. Again, collectively, we understand this is a science fiction like task. We will answer what questions we can, but please understand, there is still a vast amount we do not know, but we will be completely honest with you with regard to what we do know. We also understand that the President will be delivering an emergency broadcast this evening."

Isabella then added, "This is extremely critical to understand, what we are instituting is not a cure. Currently there is no cure or vaccine for this viral entity. This is an *engineered* virus, we recommend from an international security standpoint, that a system be developed whereby the frequencies, once they have been encoded into the radar systems, they have a specific time duration tagged to them. In other words, those frequencies, once entered, are permanently irretrievable, once they have been used for their respective purpose, they are coded to be automatically deleted from the radar generator and the generator itself be unrectifiably destroyed. There will be select individuals that will form international teams who have been screened at the highest levels to carry out the coding, and ultimate destruction of the UHF/EHF generators."

# Chapter 60

"LADIES AND GENTLEMEN, I come to you tonight," the President said, "to bring a message of hope in these times of anguish and despair. This afternoon, I authorized Dr. Isabella Kitchen, Dr. Aniru Conteh and Dr. Chidinma Kitchen to execute their plans to halt the advancement of the plague that has taken so many countless lives. These physicians have been working in the trenches of discovering a way to bring this viral menace under control. They have been part of the discovery process from the very beginning of it rearing its ugly and destructive head. But... through their tenacious, dedicated, and courageous work, they have found a way of curtailing the virus's further lethality. I ask you, the American people, for your full and complete cooperation with public health and government officials. The details of which will be forth coming as rapidly as the governments of our precious world can assemble the extraordinary logistics of this task. Please understand, that given what we are undertaking, and with the election rapidly coming upon us, I again do not believe that this is the time to completely disrupt this administration and the task before us, therefore, I cannot see with good conscience any solution to this other than, by presidential decree, order the election to be postponed until such a time that we have both this massive operation untaken and completed and this viral pestilence be brought under control. Please understand, I do this for the sake of our country, for the sake of the world's people and I believe, I *truly* believe, God has been directing the hearts and minds of Dr's Kitchen and Conteh, were it not for these brilliant and dedicated individuals I would not be able to make this announcement. When I have further information, I will update you immediately. I expect things to move rapidly from this point on.

"In addition, I have given Dr's Kitchen and Conteh full, direct and complete authorization to carry out any necessary actions to bring about resolution to the current medical crisis. This authority is authorized under Article II, Section 2, Clause 1, of The Commander in Chief Clause, of The Constitution of the United States. God's speed to Dr. Isabella Kitchen, Dr. Aniru Conteh and Dr. Chidinma Kitchen. God bless the people of the United States and of the world at large, thank you, ladies and gentlemen." Aniru, Isabella and Chidinma watched the President's address. Isabella looked at Aniru and Chidinma and simply said, "Jesus!"

# Chapter 61

THE MOST EXPEDITIOUS WAY of setting up the jetways was to use existing structures and retooling them to accommodate EHF generators. The jetways are designed to act as a means of moving large numbers of people from one point to another. They can also be quickly modified. Jetway manufacturers were contacted to provide the United States government, as well as those abroad, with all their inventory. They were to be transported to a central location within twenty-four hours. There they were transported to Brooks Air Force Base for modification.

The priority for initial placement was every emergency room in the country. And of those ERs, the hospitals within the highest population density and those reporting the greatest number of deaths associated with the outbreak. Then in a concentric circle, placement of the skyways would be outward from the center of the circle. An average jetway can accommodate at least one hundred people at one time. Once the group of people were in the jetway, they would be given a thirty-second exposure of the coded EHF. The only possible side effect was the possibility of a headache or histamine reaction due to the potential activation of mast cells, which in turn, release histamine as an inflammatory response. That's what the handouts said. Many people were skeptical that the government wasn't trying to kill them. "Hell..." one doctor said, "Even *if* the government was trying to kill you it would be better than dying from the damn virus... They could just wait, and you'd be dead soon enough anyway, dumb asses..."

It took less than forty-eight hours to set up and begin dosing people from continents and countries with the largest population densities. Europe, Russia, South America, China, Canada, Africa,

Australia, New Zeeland... Modified jetways and shipping containers were supplied to every other country. There were no political barriers that prevented or impeded access.

In about two months, the deaths from 666 started to show a decline. It was slight, but its advancement was slowing.

When the decline of the number of cases was confirmed, the President delivered an emergency address, "My fellow Americans, tonight, for the first time since this tragedy struck, I can report that the work of Drs Kitchen and Conteh has borne fruit. As you can see on this chart, the reporting of new cases is declining. This particular chart represents only the United States. But, as we speak, each of my respective Heads of State are delivering the same message to their people. We are far from being out of danger, but we are clearly on the right track and will continue to maintain our trajectory of attacking this disease. I commend and continue to pray for those involved in the ongoing eradication of this disease... As I was writing the words that I wanted to say to you, I thought about what I could say that would offer you hope, but... I wanted to finally be able to give you more than hope, I wanted to give you the results of the aggressive action *my* administration has taken to bring about, finally, *finally*, the road sign that we are moving forward in the right direction."

# THE AFTERMATH

# Chapter 62

IT WAS NOW ONE year since the scourge had begun. Approximately one-half of the earth's peoples had been killed. Many of the major cities resembled ghost towns while other smaller towns, especially in the northwestern part of the United States, and the smaller towns and cities of other countries, had faired the best throughout the crisis, meaning having the lowest body counts. Most shelves were bare of food, goods had sat and rotted, except canned goods, of course. Bagged bread was hard and covered with thick green mold. Milk had long expired and solidified. People locked themselves inside, rightfully terrified to leave their homes. Even with the mandatory EHF jetway exposure, the Army had to force hundreds of thousands of people to comply. Some people had to be shot, as they became ill-tempered and noncompliant when they boarded the *compliance busses*. Once on a CB, as they became known, the doors were locked and the entire bus load of people entered a jetway, exposed to the EHF, and then returned to their pickup point, where they were released, and a new group was picked up. This went on twenty-four hours a day, seven days a week, continually.

The soldiers wearing masks were often unconvincing that the EHF was going to save lives and eventually eradicate this fucking thing. Hospitals all had skeleton staffs, at least those doctors and nurses who had managed not to become infected and die. Manufacturing had completely ceased, and imports and exports were nonexistent. Looting had been rampant, but most looters had succumbed to the 666 long before they had time to enjoy their spoils of the plague. It was the aftermath of a viral catastrophe. People had starved and killed each other for what food there was. Some tried to form what they called *persistence communities*. But, when the subsistence waned, allies became foes, the persistence degenerated into a seared madness. Most ended up killing each other.

The Army was tasked with not only enforcing EHF compliance, but also with dispatching those to the next world, who were obviously too far gone for any cessation of the viruses' actions to be halted or were in the throes of a macabre cessation of existence. Even when the sun broke through the clouds, the gloom still shone. The news was still on air, more or less anyway. Anchors stayed at the stations and broadcast the latest news updates and exhibited their anxiety with each presidential address, fearing that it would be that progress in halting the spread of the virus had abated. It would ultimately take countless years to recover.

The President said with each broadcast that he was *not* able to reinstate elections as the state of emergency was still upon us. He was meeting with his cabinet regularly and they concurred. Plus, now that there was ongoing and a continued reduction in the body count and new cases, he had launched the most in-depth internal investigation into the originating source of the virus and how it could it have happened. The President also said at the end of each broadcast that, "The First Lady and I send our thoughts and prayers from our family to yours. May God bless America."

One of the central things a politician learns is that after any disaster or mass casualty, he must say that he is sending thoughts and prayers, and finally, close his remarks with *May God Bless America*. Somehow that seems to negate the rest of the world. Sports teams have their prayer huddle before each game, especially those where there is an enormous financial payoff. When Isabella heard broadcasts of either politicians or sports teams, she wondered if God had a preference, either politically or team wise?

# Chapter 63

ISABELLA, ANIRU AND CHIDINMA had managed to relocate to a small village in southern British Columbia. Along the way Aniru and Isabella had decided to get married. They crossed the border in Eureka, Montana. There were no border guards on either side when they crossed. It took about ten hours or so to hit Lillooet, BC.

The town was originally an 1850s goldrush boom town, that, like all boom towns, lost its thunder when the gold was mined out. Now it had a couple thousand people and a good number of *St'at'imc* (Salish) Native Americans. There was also the Lillooet Hospital. And, most amazingly, there had not been one case of the 666. Once the crisis began to blow up, the community shut down the majority of flights into their small community airport and set up barriers to prevent the train from coming through on its twice weekly run. Trucks bearing supplies had *'stop and go'* points where the driver would pull up and his trailer unloaded by locals. He wasn't permitted to get out of the truck and his windows had to remain up, then the driver was waved on. A few drivers were shot when they refused to stay in their truck cabs. Given that Lillooet was hell to get to, it was prone to harsh winters and certainly not much to do, the virus had miraculously not yet encroached into the community.

Isabella, Aniru and Chidinma were unsure how they would be received when they pulled into town. But... it wasn't long before they were all pulling shifts at the hospital. When the mayor found out who they were, he took them to the hospital CEO who gave them privileges on the spot. The town had a few good size hunting cabins that weren't being hunted from, so the mayor made an 'executive decision' to let them use a couple for as long as they stayed in Lillooet. Even with the apocalyptic devastation throughout the world, they found, at least for a time, Lillooet a reprieve from the madness.

And yet... as time went on, they couldn't continue to ignore the lies and fabrications that the President was making. He was responsible for this tragedy and now was presenting himself as a savior. Isabella said he would do virtually anything to stay in power. Aniru continued Isabella's thought, saying that "the President had redefined the word *anything*."

When Isabella had asked what had happened to Prokiv, the President simply said, "He has transitioned into another assignment."

Shortly after their initial meeting at USAMRIID, Isabella, Aniru and Chidinma had been relieved of their official duties. Those now being turned over to the Army command. It was then that they decided to find, at least temporarily, someplace out of harm's way and more sedate, to try and come to terms with what they had been through and how they wanted their lives to be in the future. For now, Lillooet was that place.

That changed about three months after they arrived, when the President of the United States delivered his "Last..." message to the American people about the pandemic, in which he added at the end... "Ladies and Gentlemen of the United States, we have reached the end of pandemic. It has been a devastating time for our country and for the world. There is no way to express the gratitude to the thankless heroes who sacrificed of themselves for the good of their country. As we now have entered the final phase of recovery, I am continuing the moratorium on elections, likely this will extend through the next decade, until the economy and the infrastructure, which has deteriorated significantly, are restored. I am also ordering a cash subsidy, of yet an indeterminate amount, to each family, to begin the process of rebuilding their lives. These checks will go out within the next thirty-days. Obviously, this amount will strike many as unmanageable by my government, but the people of America have been put through hell on earth. It is imperative that my government now stands up for you."

Isabella and Aniru had reached their level of tolerance. The President, even though he typically referred to *his* cabinet, no one knew who besides him, who was actually running the government. But, most importantly, the President now referred to the government as "*my*..." Which he certainly wasn't using as a euphemism. Isabella noted, he was buying off the American people. "...Create a disaster, declare yourself the *only* one who can *resolve* the disaster, block any opposition that may arise and then buy off what has become your indoctrinated constituency, and always, *always*, count on and support the ignorant desperation of the masses." Aniru said the same thing, though without the pandemic, had occurred in South Africa. "This President chose to use a different kind of virulence against the people of the U.S., a *viral* apartheid."

"Of course, how can he possibly he stopped?" Isabella pondered. It was then that she thought about something they still had in their possession. Something that may at least bring about some questions about how the government, namely the President and Dr. Prokiv, conceived and executed the entire genocide. "I think it is time for us to leave here..." Isabella said. Aniru agreed.

When they told Chidinma about their decision, she said she would be staying. At least for the near future. She had become involved in the chase to help her mother and Aniru to find the Popobawa and now, after the time in Lillooet, Chidinma wanted to find her own way in the world. It took two weeks for Isabella and Aniru to leave Lillooet and reenter the U.S. Much of their discussion on the way back was how no one would believe what the origin was of the 666 and the catastrophe it had caused. In truth, Isabella and Aniru were coming to terms with their own disbelief. The entire odyssey was as though they had spent the time in the nether world. Nor would, as they had discussed before, anyone believe that the President's plan was to install himself as *President for Life*. Aniru said it reminded him of, "Papa Doc, of Haiti. The problem with fucking dictators," Isabella said, "... is that they always get *hung*, either, in reality or metaphorically. But they're so goddamn infused with unfettered megalomania, that they can't see it, even when they are hanging upside down in the middle of the square. It's like someone destroyed their ability to look back at themselves and see their ultimate fate." Aniru responded, "With their last breath, they say, '*how can you do this, how can you not love me.*'" It was right about then that they crossed the Canada/U.S. border.

They still had their farm outside of Atlanta. After more than a year of being gone and days of driving, Isabella and Aniru were beginning to pull the sheets off their furniture and readying to sleep in their own bed.

# Chapter 64

THE PRESIDENT HAD NOT emerged from Cheyanne Mountain for more than a year. Now, on the flight back to Washington, he was returning triumphant. He knew Prokiv had thought he was playing him for a fool. But *he* selected Prokiv and pandered to Prokiv's belief that *he* was the orchestrator of the plan. "You always choose loners, if you can, to begin something that will end up with *their* demise, that way no one gives a damn when they disappear," the President thought as they began their descent. A crowd had been carefully selected. There was a raucous greeting awaiting him at the airport.

He left Washington as an unadorned president at the height of the emerging pandemic, to save the country and *now... now* he returned as a *plurimarum palmarum gladiator*, who was forced into the arena to go up against a vicious leviathan. "*Jesus*, I can do no wrong..." the President thought as he deplaned and stepped onto the tarmac.

# Chapter 65

So much was disorganized, which ultimately was what the President wanted. That way it is much harder to put in place a real structure to investigate anything about the scourge. In a few weeks he began issuing executive orders disrupting departments of the government that could in any way threaten his newly, albeit ill-defined, *Paladin* for the people. He was also lauded by dignitaries and heads of foreign governments as the one who brought about the end to the calamity that shook the world. Religious leaders praise him as the leader needed at the time and likely delivered to the earth by God. One church leader while at the pulpit went so far as to say during his sermon, "...And on this day, this day of thanks, we praise *him*, yes we praise *him*... But *him* is not our Lord and Savior but our President, who the Almighty delivered to us, to champion and end to the plague. On this day of celebration, *he* has brought us together once again."

There was a rush by members of Congress to name whatever monument, public statue, or government entity after him. It was a self-instillment. In a few years he "...would allow elections to begin again," the President said. But... who would dare be foolish enough to run against him?

The papers had begun publishing again. A few journalists were beginning to, or at least attempting to, investigate the origins of 666 and how such a tragedy could have occurred. The papers that had the audacity to entertain such questions were scorned by the administration. And, in a short time, their subscriptions, just beginning to rise after the plague, began falling again. Not long after that, layoffs and closures began.

It wasn't long after the layoffs that a document arrived at the six largest newspapers in the United States, papers in Paris, Berlin, Shanghai, Moscow, and Toronto. The same document also arrived at the major television media outlets worldwide. It was copies of a wrinkled treatise, from one Khalid Amaechi, Ph.D., attesting to the fact that the 666 was developed under the authority and auspices of the President of the United States and a scientist named Dr. Theodore Prokiv, the document also acknowledged that it was developed *specifically* as a biological weapon. The original document was sent to the Speaker of the House.

A secondary document accompanied the material from Dr. Amaechi. This revealed that the President and Dr. Prokiv conspired to infect certain populations to induce intentional selective culling. "Thinning..." the document said, was what Dr. Prokiv called it. "... Necessary to reverse the trend that had developed toward population and interrace expansion. Soon there will be a rationing of resources, those that can afford them and have access to them should not be hampered by those who cannot. Some, actually many, human beings are nothing more dregs of and on a society that has to continually fight against it. Things have simply gotten out of control..." A "*thank you*" was delivered to one of Dr. Prokiv's former students, who kept copious notes and who had been appalled at his early assertions.

There were news bulletins, headlines and... disbelief. "This *has* to be science fiction," one news caster broadcast.

The congress initially disavowed the story and declared the documents forgeries. "A mad plot to unseat the President who brought about the cessation to one of the greatest calamities ever to strike the earth."

The problem was that each denial fell apart. Each representative had family members who had perished. Of course, many congressional members themselves succumbed too. The world had changed, as had the tolerance for lies and deception.

In a short while the International Criminal Court issued warrants for the arrest of the President of the United States and Dr. Theodore Prokiv, for Crimes Against Humanity and Genocide. The United States refused to recognize the ICC warrant, "...Although we are a member nation of the ICC, we believe recognition of the warrant would impede continued recovery." In a few weeks after the ICC issued the warrant, the President resigned from office.

At exactly one minute after the Vice President was sworn in as

President, he issued a full and blanket pardon of the President. "It isn't complicated." he said, "We... at all costs, must put this behind us... regardless of what any nation, or judiciary seeks, *we* decide the fate of our own. That is all I will say on the matter." Dr. Prokiv was never found, although rumors were that he had absconded to Bolivia.

The now former President and his family were given a compound at one of the governments undisclosed locations. Most of the government's locations were undisclosed. Many were underground or compounds within compounds. During WWII most AF bases had complete tunnel systems beneath them. Those had been expanded and turned into cities within themselves. The former president would simply be given what he needed as time went on. He knew too much. Regardless of his own sins, he knew of too many sins of other governmental officials also. It was better to have granted him a pardon than to risk having what he knew become a bargaining chip. The now former President knew everything there was to know about what remained under lock and key or what the American people had been lied to about for a hundred years. The former President made it his business to know. Some men collected money, he collected information. The greatest currency of all. When he was younger, he read a novel about an assassin who went to a gunsmith with plans for a specifically designed sniper's rifle. At the end of their negotiations the assassin said, "Of course, once our transaction is complete, you will have never heard of me." The bespectacled gunsmith looked at the assassin and said, "Oh but yes. As protection for myself, as you might imagine, I must assure myself of some form of security. I have buried in a place that exists in my mind information about my *very* private clientele, and that location resides with one person in another part of the world. Upon my *natural* death, the contents will be removed and destroyed. Of course, should my death be, say from *unnatural* causes, then of course the disposal of the information would be a far different matter." *Détente.*

# Chapter 66

Isabella and Aniru settled into their country place. Isabella still taught and consulted as did Aniru. They were both considered the world's foremost experts on rare and yet unidentified diseases.

They were never questioned as to where the leak came from that had brought down the President and exposed what he and Prokiv had launched against humanity. During her lectures she would often discuss the implications of combining different disease entities. "Christ..." she would add, typically at the end of her lecture, "...We don't know ultimately what we are in for in the future. Humanity was but a few billion people from being wiped from the face of the earth. I remember as a child both of my parents were physicians in Kentucky, and both fought the goddamn coal companies, who treated miners like chattel. There was a book on my mother's shelf, *Germ Warfare, The Coming Threat*... I was fascinated by it, but at the end, the author wrote, '*However, this can never happen as there are too many good scientists with good judgment and most importantly good moral standing to do such a thing...*' When I was in my residency, I happened to visit my parents and again found this book. I thumbed to the last page and again read that last sentence, and I thought, humm, go tell that to the Indians.

"Whether or not the next pandemic is caused by some heinous bastard or whether it finds its way out of the jungle on the back of a Lukolela swamp rat, because someone, somewhere decided they wanted a very rare rodent as a pet, and... It is going to happen. If we continue to not be prepared, in terms of putting the necessary funding into detection and treatments, then we could be looking at a viral asteroid hurling toward the earth. Let me just mention also, once life of some form is found interstellarly, then God knows what we will be up against and I also guarantee you, this *too* will happen." It was rare when one of Isabella's lectures were not packed. Typically, they were promoted up to a year in advance.

She and Aniru, more than anything, loved their small farm. Aniru, from being raised in Sierra Leone, knew as much about farming as he did medicine. Both he and Isabella decided that they had seen enough death and became vegetarians. "Isn't it interesting, Isabella, when we are lecturing or talking with someone, they just want to know about what we did during the pandemic, or rare diseases, but in our day-to-day lives they could care less. They don't want to talk about it, and they certainly don't want to read about it. We could write two books, one on the pandemic and one on our lives here on the farm ...which do you think would sell and which would disappear the day it was published?" They also had a habit of fucking outside, at least when the bugs weren't biting.

The CDC would periodically call upon either or both when something came up in the world that required their expertise. But... for the most part, their heroism, as the former president called it, was forgotten over time.

The pandemic became a footnote for historians in the future to investigate, though some now sought to interview the isolated President, but every request was denied. The hope was that at least one interview would take place before he died. But, ultimately, none would.

# Chapter 67

IN THE MIDDLE OF February, Aniru received a call from the Health Minister of Sierra Leone. It had started again. Another outbreak of Lassa Fever. "Yes, Dr. Conteh, the mortality of Lassa is supposed to be only one percent, but, as you know, those are statistics on a page, calculated by dry, unemotional equations that can't take into account immune systems ravaged by starvation and constant dysentery due to horrid sanitation and contaminated drinking water. During the civil war, you were the *only* physician in the world who had the knowledge and dedication to save our country men. You sir, *you*, were homeless yourself and at times, I know... starving yourself, and *yet* you saved thousands upon thousands during the war. Would it be possible, sir, for you to come to our aid once again. Lassa is killing our people again. We are trying but we can't get ahead of it, if you could come, it would be of great benefit to us."

That night Aniru spoke to Isabella and said he wanted to go. The CDC certainly could have called upon him but rarely did so. He taught here and there but... his mother country had asked for his assistance. "I don't think it will take very long." If there was anyone who would understand, it would be Isabella. Three days later, and after seventeen hours in the air, Dr. Aniru Conteh landed in Freetown.

He was picked up by the health minister who drove him to the Kenema Government Hospital, mostly a group of primitive concrete buildings, encircled by a gravel courtyard. The ward had not been told of his coming. When he walked onto the floor, there were gasps. Aniru Conteh, MD, was known as the *Great Healer*. As he made his way through the L-Ward, the two other doctors and the few nurses began to realize who was going to be taking charge of the floor, simply bowed when he walked by. Of course, one may ask, why would they think Dr. Conteh would be taking charge, but, of course, how could they not.

Supplies of the antiviral that was used off label to try and quell the early symptoms of Lassa and give the body at least a chance to use its immune system to fight the disease and prevent it from entering the mortality stage were limited. The Lassa Virus, in other parts of the world, is handled in a BSL-4 lab, there was no such lab in Sierra Leone. There weren't even any antiviral protective covering that were remotely adequate to prevent physicians and nurses from contracting the virus. And yet they worked on and treated patients every day. Typically, whenever there is an outbreak of a hemorrhagic fever, physicians, and nurses, other than the patients themselves, are the first to die from exposure to the disease.

The early symptoms are fever and headaches, followed by abdominal upset. It isn't long before the beginnings of vascular leakage occur. Then in the final stages, it is as though a damn, holding back a torrent of blood, bursts... and then the victim of Lassa excruciatingly exsanguinates.

Aniru began to segregate the patients just beginning to show symptoms from those in the mid to later stages of the disease. He ordered all but a few of the antiviral in Sierra Leone be brought to the Lassa Ward. Some doses were left in each location, maintaining at least a few vials, in case there was an outbreak in that section of the country. "Christ, no one is interested in this disease, the only thing that anyone gives a damn about is that Lassa stays where it is. A Lassa outbreak in London would be like building a junkyard in the middle of mansion row," Aniru would say over and over, again and again, in countless different ways. One day while he and one of the nurses were walking the ward, the nurse asked, "Why do we give the patients the antiviral when there's so little of it and there is no treatment that is effective?" To which Aniru replied, "Because it offers them something besides euthanasia, the antiviral takes the edge off just a bit. How could we deny them?" Then he would remember his many conversations with Isabella about how certain populations of people are thought of as write-offs and then thinking about the global 666 tragedy.

Patients in their final hours were kept sedated. Yet even in sedation they writhed in pain. Once a Lassa patient entered the hospital, their family could no longer come and see them. The doctors and nurses did their best to see that no patient died alone. The constant risk of being infected themselves hovered over them like the Sword of Damocles.

In the middle of March, a pregnant nurse came to the Lassa ward. She was well into the last stage of her life, consumed by Lassa. Aniru wondered how she was still alive, as blood was even coming out of her tear ducts. When Aniru placed his stethoscope against her abdomen, he couldn't detect a fetal heartbeat. The baby was dead, likely it had bled out in the womb. He wanted to get a liver enzyme panel, which would tell him if she was in complete hepatic failure, and if so, it would mean she had about twenty-four hours to live. As he began to insert the needle into her arm, the nurse began to have a seizure. Her arms became tonic right as Aniru inserted the needle into her vein. The tip of the needle tore through the skin and pricked the index finger of his left hand. Because of the low viscosity of the nurse's blood, the tip of the needle was saturated with blood when it punctured Aniru's finger, exposing him to Lassa. He grabbed a squeeze bottle of bleach solution and soaked the site of the stick. It was clear to him that when the needle came out of her vein and pricked him, it was covered in her blood. Reality now overshadowed denial. Aniru had been exposed to Lassa.

That night he called Isabella and explained what had happened. Of course, they both knew the implications. Isabella thought of their medical specialty in the way that she had grown up with, hearing stories of miners' wives, sending their men off to dig deep in the earth, with their dinner pails in hand. They always packed a bit extra in the pail, "just in case..." they would say, something "dudn't go right down there..." they'd at least have a bite to eat while they were "waitin for help to come." If the miner came up alright, then he'd give what little his wife had packed extra for him to their youngins. Isabella once told Aniru that the miners' wives said a mine disaster was caused by an unhappy Tommy Knocker, "They're like a pissed-off leprechaun. The wives of the miners would rotate baking a small saffron cake every week, which the miner would leave behind in the hole, to make the Tommy Knocker happy, before he came back up at the end of his shift." Right before they hung up, Aniru said to Isabella, "I must have pissed off a Tommy Knocker." Isabella responded, "I will call

Chidinma, and we will get there as soon as we can get a flight out."

After they hung up, Isabella called Chidinma. She was still in Canada. In less than an hour, Chidinma had left Lillooet and was heading to Spokane. In about eight hours she arrived at the Spokane airport. The flight to Atlanta took five hours. The next day, Isabella and Chidinma were in the air and on their way to Sierra Leone. As the nose of the plane rotated, Isabella recalled 1 Corinthians 15:56-58, "...*The prick of death.*" It had now been three days since Aniru called Isabella.

# Chapter 68

WHEN THEY ARRIVED AT the Kenema Government Hospital, Aniru was already beginning to experience headaches, chills, and fever. Isabella and Chidinma had packed disposable personal protective suits. He was in a room by himself, nurses were going in and out of his room constantly. As soon as Isabella and Chidinma arrived, they gowned up and went to be with him. Aniru was sweating profusely, the nurses at his bedsides were applying cool compresses and slipping chips of ice between his cracked lips. Isabella ordered an antiviral be given to Aniru.

During the next thirty-six hours, Aniru began hemorrhaging from multiple orifices and increasingly becoming delirious. As Isabella looked at Aniru, she thought that his lips, that she had once kissed so passionately, now looked like a gaping wound. His fever was peeking out at 41c. Aniru was on fire. Isabella and Chidinma took over Aniru's primary care. One week after first being pricked and passing through the critical survival stage of Lassa, Aniru was beginning to show signs that he would survive. His fever had come down to within a few points of Hg of being normal. But most importantly the bleeding, except for a few ml here and there, had come to an end. Aniru was sitting up, talking, and taking small amounts of food. Isabella and Chidinma had decided it was safe to care for Aniru without being covered in protective gear.

Two weeks after the initial finger stick, Isabella was sitting by his side. Aniru looked over at her and said, "Isabella, I am so tired. So tired..." He reached up to touch her face and she saw that his hand was swollen. Isabella pulled back the cover and Aniru's feet were swollen too. Later that evening Chidinma checked his urine bag. There was less than four ounces. Aniru was becoming increasingly confused and drifting off to sleep, continuously after being awakened. Isabella pulled a blood sample and found that he was in a state of hypoalbuminemia, with an albumin level of 2.5g/dL and was hyperkalemic with a potassium level was 7.5mEq/L. In a few hours Aniru was beginning to labor for breath.

As Isabella and Chidinma sat with Aniru, he was passing in and out of consciousness. When Isabella looked into Aniru's dark brown eyes, she wondered if he could still see her. She looked at Chidinma and said, "Aniru always sees everything, I wonder if he can see the eternal heartache in my eyes?" Chidinma tearfully nodded.

Mostly now, Isabella and Chidinma glanced back and forth at each other, but spoke little toward the end.

Isabella realized there was no language that was capable of expressing the depth of grief that gets birthed, as one who is loved so much is dying. She remembered as a child going to funerals of miners in Paintsville, who had died during a mine collapse. Their wives would be hanging onto the side of the casket, screaming, "...Oh Lord Jesus... no...!" While others would walk alongside the coffin and shake their heads, some passed out, once a wife jumped into the grave before her husband's casket was interred. But... no matter what was said or not said, no matter how who was left behind, absolutely nothing was adequate. "Christ..." Isabella thought, "What does *adequate* even mean?"

And now she and Chidinma sat and watched as the man who they loved in completely different but equally deep ways began entering eternity. Aniru's breathing was deep and labored, *Kussmaul* breathing came up from her memory and crept into her conscious. And when it did, Isabella wished in that moment she wasn't a physician. And then, not long after, the death rattles began.

Chidinma looked at Isabella and said, "They're not the death rattles, but the *rattles* of death. God is sitting quiet, and death is announcing *it* has arrived."

Word had spread that Aniru was ill, that Lassa had come for him. People were coming from Freetown and from the surrounding villages. News was spreading like a bush fire in a drought. When Isabella and Chidinma came out of Aniru's room, they saw doctors, nurses, and patients, some knowing that death would soon leave Aniru's room and come into theirs. But they too were swallowed up by grief.

The city of Kenema within hours of hearing of his death seemingly came to a standstill. *Aniru Conteh, MD* was not only Isabella's husband and Chidinma's chosen father, but he also belonged to his country. Sierra Leone had few heroes, Aniru was one. For weeks on end, the news everyday said something about what "Dr. Conteh," had done for Sierra Leone and its people. The governor of Sierra Leone said, "Dr. Conteh was the world's foremost expert on Lassa fever... we hope and pray that his work and dedication continues and that the people of West Africa are not forgotten..."

As Isabella and Chidinma began boarding for their flight back to the United States, they stood at the entrance of the plane, turned around and thought of everything they had been through. Isabella looked at Chidinma and softly said, "A fucking needle prick..."

# Chapter 69

It had been two months since Aniru's death. Isabella had gone into isolation. Not a depressive isolation, but a time of deciding how she wanted to spend the remainder of her time on earth. Chidinma too was at a time of contemplation in her life. The world was different now. Million's dead, governments ruptured and some completely collapsed.

The three of them had seen and been part of the most devastating mass loss of life since the black plague and yet... the deaths were so vast in numbers as to be anonymous. But... those hours with Aniru dying, moment by moment, the man she knew descending deeper and deeper into oblivion, to where who he was, was no longer known to him but only to those who loved him. In the end, the dying cedes the essence of their being to the living.

# THE LAST AFTERMATH

# Chapter 70

It took about seven hours for Isabella and Chidinma to get there. They had left before sunrise that morning and pulled in about four that afternoon. Isabella had contacted the hospital's Medical Staff Office a few weeks before and applied for full privileges for her and Chidinma. On that initial call, the secretary at the medical staff office realized who Isabella was. "Oh, my golly Ned! Why this just can't be... Now are you sure, honey, you're who you are sayin' you are and you're not joshin' me?" Isabella assured her that she was really who she said she was and that she and Chidinma would be arriving in town sometime in the next month or so and she wanted to get their staff privileges set up before they arrived.

When they pulled into Paintsville, Isabella drove directly to The Spencer Duty, Jr. Research Center for Black Lung Disease, the SDRC. "Chidinma, Spencer Duty, Jr. was your great grandfather. Even though you were not of his blood, it wouldn't have mattered to him in any way. He would have been *so* proud of you. I can see him dancing in the street. Spencer Duty, Jr. funded this research center and wanted it named after my parents, Moses Kitchen and Janice McGarrity, but after he died, they had it renamed for him. You know your grandfather was one of the first physicians to perform a Hemicorporectomy off of the battlefield. The patient lived for many years after the surgery, actually he lived at the hospital. The surgery was how your grandfather and grandmother met. Something about her coming around the corner in the recovery ward and seeing the patient cut in half and asked who in the hell did *that*!!! I guess dad was pretty taken with my mother... Likely the only prematrimonial meeting like that in history... The patient used to ride around the hospital on a motorized cart, that facility engineering made for him. The SDRC is now considered one of the world's top research facilities on black lung and toxic related respiratory disease."

Chidinma looked over at Isabella, "Do you think we will be welcomed, especially me?"

Isabella reached over and touched Chidinma on the shoulder, "My mother and father didn't just treat black lung, they treated everything and everyone. A lot of times they got paid by pots of chicken and dumplings from folks who'd killed their last chicken for them. So many of the people around here don't have anything, not two nickels to rub together. To this day, I don't know how they made their practice work, I know they got money from my grandfather, but they didn't even have someone in their office who billed patients. I don't know if *any* patient ever got a bill from them. They were on staff at the hospital, so they got paid through them, but really, I just don't know. *But...* I do know they were *revered* in Paintsville and in an area about five miles from here, Van Lear Junction. So, we come in with that kind of good wind at our back. I think you will find that most of the patients will be color blind. And, my dear daughter, you will see things here you would *never* see in Atlanta."

As Isabella and Chidinma were walking up to the front door of the SDRC, a blaring whistle began warbling and then... the sirens. "Christ," Isabella, looking alarmed said. "We have to get to the hospital ER to help. There's been a disaster at one of the mines. Welcome to Paintsville, Chidinma!" As they made their way to the hospital ER, Isabella, seemingly out of nowhere, thought, "I haven't got my period yet..."

# Acknowledgement

*MEDICAL PERSONNEL AND EPIDEMIOLOGISTS in the farthest reaches of the world are on the front lines of disease outbreaks. These men and women are often confronted by the unknown. And, that unknown can be life threatening to them and to the rest of us. Their names are rarely brought forth, but their dedication to the work of discovering the threat of new diseases can never be discounted.*

www.ingramcontent.com/pod-product-compliance
Lightning Source LLC
Chambersburg PA
CBHW031955010726
47493CB00007B/2205